Shanghai Gold

Shanghai Gold

Thomas Sturm

Shanghai Gold
ISBN: 978-0-9786081-0-1

Published by Upsurge Books

www.upsurgebooks.com
www.shanghaigold.net

This is a work of fiction. All the characters and events
portrayed in the book are fictional and any resemblance
to real people or incidents is purely coincidental.

First Edition: September 2010 (v9.3)

For Kazumi

Thanks to
Chris Baty and nanowrimo.org
for the inspiration

Many thanks to my beta readers
Diana, Yoko, Greg, Thomas, Paul,
Michelle, Darren, Loïc, Lori and Jan-Marie

1

THE BLANK PAPER was silently gliding through the clear developer fluid. Shapes appeared. There was a window. The shadow of a man on a bed in front of it. More and more of the photo became visible while the developer did its work, revealing details in stark contrast in the red light of the darkroom.

It was the photo of a man lying on a bed, peaceful and relaxed. Sunlight came through a window behind the bed, showing a busy river scene with sampans and steamships, sails flying and smoke drifting in the wind.

The man was lying on his back and had a knife sticking in his breast.

"Shit!"

Dean jerked back with a gasp. He suddenly felt cold. He had spent several hours in the darkroom and he was not sure if he could trust his eyes. The only thing he could hear was his rapid breathing and the relentless hum of the air conditioner. He willed his heart to slow down and bent back over the developer tub.

Yes, this man clearly had been murdered. Or this photo was a very sick joke, frozen on a strip of film for at least the last five decades.

The film had come from a vintage camera that Dean had bought on eBay a few weeks ago and he had not expected to find anything but a few smiling family pictures on the film that had been forgotten in the camera for more than half a century.

DEAN DROPPED THE picture into the fixer tub and went back to the workbench to print the rest of the pictures when the phone rang. It sounded unnaturally loud to Dean, his subconscious half-expecting the dead man's ghost to jump out from behind the film storage shelves.

"Hello?"

"Am I speaking to Dean Lashure?" a female voice asked.

"Yes. Who is this?" Dean was not expecting any callers on his office phone late at night.

"My... my name is Karen. Karen Chadbourne. You don't know me... but you have something that is very important to me."

Dean thought she spoke like she was in a hurry – or as if she had been running. Her voice was attractive and he was about to create a picture of her in his mind when what she had said hit him like an electric shock. He had been facing the old-fashioned wall phone in his darkroom, but now he turned around, looking at the picture of the dead man on the table.

"What do you mean? Are you sure you have the right number?"

He wanted to play for more time. He had to think about what was going on. She had to be talking about the camera.

"It's about a camera -" Her voice had turned into a whisper. "I know you bought a camera at an online auction... I have been trying to contact you for more than a week. I... I can pay you back. I really need the camera back. It is a family heirloom."

So much for what she wanted. Dean wasn't sure how to handle this situation. She clearly knew that he had bought the camera, but how had she been tracking him down?

"Uhm... Listen, I want to think about this. Can I call you back?"

"We can meet later – I am in San Francisco now." She said with a sigh.

"You came to San Francisco because of this camera?"

There was silence on the other end. Dean almost thought she had hung up.

"Y... yes. Can we meet later? I'm staying in the Hilton near Union Square – we can meet somewhere here in the city."

Dean was intrigued. He was not used to women begging to meet with him. "OK, you win. There is a café on the ground floor of your Hotel, I think it's called... Kazumi's or something like that. I will see you there..." He realized how late it was. "At ten o'clock – in half an hour."

"The café on the ground floor at ten. I will be there."

"OK, see you then."

"Wait! How will I recognize you?"

"Well – you found me here, right? I don't think you'll have trouble finding me in a small café. Oh – and I will be the only one with a Kodak Medalist on the table."

"Oh! OK, I see you then!" She had cheered up considerably.

DEAN LASHURE STEPPED back to the dryer line and hung the picture of the dead man up to dry, all his movements on automatic while his mind was busy reviewing his conversation with Karen Chadbourne.

The phone rang again. Dean went the two steps back to the wall phone and picked up on the second ring.

"Hello."

"..."

"Hello? Who is this?" Dean waited for several more seconds and then hung up. This was odd. He looked back at the work bench where the roll of ancient middle format film from the vintage Kodak camera was snaking around a box of photo paper. He would have loved to see the rest of the photos, but his impulsive reaction to meet with that woman in half an hour made it impossible.

HE SWITCHED THE red light off and went out through the heavy double doors of the darkroom that kept the office lights out. The office was where Dean spent most of his time when he was not traveling on one of his photo assignments. The wall across from the darkroom was floor to ceiling archival boxes for his photos, to the left was a desk facing the window down to Third Street.

He was very happy with this office space. The building was quiet and safe and had a doorman at the entrance. It was a converted warehouse that had seen busy times during the dot-com boom, when all of its features had been upgraded, but now it had drastically lower rents that had made it affordable for freelancers like Dean to rent a quite respectable office for himself.

On this day Dean had come back from an assignment in Canada for a new travel magazine that was based here in San Francisco and he hoped that "The Bay Traveler" would be successful enough to keep him busy for some time. He had directly gone to the office to drop his photo gear off and to his delight had found a small box waiting for him at the office door. He regularly bought vintage photo equipment on auction sites and right now this had looked like a great way to relax.

Now the open box was sitting on his desk chair with little foam peanuts spilling to the floor and over his travel bag. The camera, a Kodak Medalist from the late 1930s, was facing Dean on the desk next to his computer, the lens staring at him. Dean realized that the last picture this lens had taken was of a dead man.

He put the heavy camera into his small backpack, grabbed his keys from the desk and left the office. He always took the stairs, since his office was only on the third floor and the the elevator was small, smelly and slow.

THE DOORMAN WAS at his tiny desk and control center with the flickering pictures of the security cameras on a small monitor.

"Good night, Tony."

"Good night, Mr Lashure."

The glass door fell heavy into its lock behind him and the fresh wind of a typical San Francisco evening removed the last of the chemical darkroom smell from his lungs. Dean walked around the corner where he always parked under the highway, loose gravel crunching under his shoes.

A dark, heavy BMW had just been parked next to his red Honda Civic and while he unlocked the door, three men came out of the other car.

"Mr. Lashure?"

Dean froze. Too many people knew who he was and where he could be found. He looked up and saw three men standing behind his car, only a few feet from the back fender. They were from Asian descent, nothing special in the cultural whirlpool that San Francisco had become in the 21st century. What was special was that they almost looked like identical triplets, even wearing identical dark blue suits. The man in the middle was more heavyset than the two wingmen and it was he who now spoke again.

"We would like to talk to you, Mr. Lashure. We have an interesting offer for you." He said with a very distinct British accent. The three men stood without movement, the two wingmen just moving their eyes to take in the surroundings.

Dean had not yet said a thing, but he had completely opened the door and slowly dropped the backpack into the car.

"Who are you?" Not his greatest line ever, but this was really the big question. He did not feel threatened yet, but the strangers looked like threats were very much a possibility if things didn't go as they liked it.

He had to relax his grip on the car door since he was about to press his fingers through the window. He became aware of the fact that under the highway and behind the office building nobody else could see what was happening.

"We represent somebody who believes that you are in possession of an antique object that belongs to him. But since you were not aware of this fact, we are authorized to pay you a quite substantial sum... How about ten thousand dollars for the Kodak camera you bought two weeks ago?"

"What? *Ten thousand?* For the camera? Who are you guys?"

The man on the right started reaching for something under his jacket. That was enough for Dean. He dived into the driver's seat, pulled the door shut behind him and slammed the key into the ignition. Flames of pain were shooting through his right leg, as he had hit the heavy camera with his knee on the way in. In the rear view mirror he could see an argument erupting with the leader of the goon squad holding the arm of the guy on the right who was now clearly holding a gun under his jacket.

The engine came alive and Dean hit the car into reverse. He saw shapes jumping out of the way, two to the left, one to the right. The tires finally found some purchase and his Civic shot backwards out of the parking lot onto Third Street. While Dean turned the car around, he saw the three guys wildly gesticulating, soon to be left behind while he drove north towards Market Street.

HE HAD TO find out what was going on. Clearly, this camera – or more accurately, the film it had sheltered for the last fifty or sixty years – contained something that was worth a lot more than the hundred dollars he had paid on eBay. Up to now he had only clearly seen one of the pictures on the roll, there were at least seven more shots he had to examine. He also had to check who he bought this camera from before he met the woman that had called – what was her name? Karen?

His hands were shaking badly and he gripped the steering wheel hard. Downtown traffic was a blur while he was thinking about what to do next.

Dean decided to drive home first before he would go to the Hilton, but his subconscious must have known all along, because he was already driving over the top of California Street, only one block away from his apartment.

He hit the brakes and rolled to a stop at the corner of his block. There were three men standing in front of his apartment, their dark blue suits almost black under the street light.

They could not possibly be the same men. Six men? There were six men looking for him? Maybe even more, he had no idea.

"OK Karen, you win."

He passed his apartment, forced himself not to look at the men out front, and turned left into Hyde Street.

HE PARKED IN the Hilton's garage since he didn't feel like walking along dark downtown streets and emerged in the lobby of the hotel. He was a few minutes late by the time he arrived at Kazumi's, but the café was empty. He ordered a Latte from the counter and balanced the cup to a small table in the corner with a good view of the entrance. He took the heavy camera out of the backpack and placed it on the table next to the Latte and waited.

A few minutes later a woman entered the café. She had dark brown hair, dark eyes and her face looked faintly Native American. She wore a dark red sweater, blue jeans and white sneakers and looked for all the world like a vacationer. She looked around the room, saw Dean and the camera on the table and came over to him like a guided missile.

"Mr. Lashure? I'm Karen Chadbourne." she tried to smile at him, but it didn't seem to work as she had expected. They shook hands. Her grip was firm and just the right length for Dean.

"Please sit down – can I get you some coffee?"

"I... no. Yes! Please." she sighed deeply "I'm sorry, but it is just so strange to see you sitting here with this camera. A hot chocolate would be nice."

Dean got up and ordered the hot chocolate. He turned around to lean on the counter while the woman behind the bar prepared the chocolate. Karen Chadbourne was sitting at the table, stiffly upright, one arm extended and softly touching the camera, like one would touch the face of a sleeping child.

She was completely lost in thought, one hand still touching the camera when Dean came back with the hot chocolate.

"Nice camera, isn't it?"

Her hand jerked back as if she had touched a hot iron. "Yes." Her tone changed like she was imitating somebody. "It is a beautiful machine. Produced back when a camera was still something special, made by craftsmen." Her voice went back to normal. "That's what my grandfather always said."

"So this was... is your grandfather's camera?"

"Yes. He bought it in 1941 in Shanghai." Dean noticed that she was uncomfortable now, but after rearranging her features in the chair, she seemed to come to a decision and continued "Listen, Mr Lashure..."

"Oh please – call me Dean."

She nodded "Karen." More moving around. Dean used the moment to look at her. She was actually very attractive, in a tomboy kind of way. Her dark hair was shoulder length and framed a round face with a cute, short nose and large dark brown eyes. She was maybe four inches shorter than Dean and had a nice figure. It looked like she was working out a lot – she had the typical small folds around the eyes and mouth that Dean always thought of as workout-wrinkles.

"So why do you want this camera back? I bought it fair and square." he was watching her face intently for a reaction.

"I knew you would ask. Believe me, I've been waiting to have this conversation for more than a week now."

She sipped from her hot chocolate, took a deep breath and continued.

"This was my grandfather's camera. He had bought it in 1941 in Shanghai where he had been living since before the war. He had a good job and he was always into photography, so he bought this camera – he splurged, as he always said when he told me about it." - she smiled, recalling her grandfather's stories - "He was already married to my grandmother at the time and they always went out into the countryside on weekends, not so much anymore at that time, since the war was already devastating China, but Granddad was hoping for better times."

"But times did not get better. It actually got a lot worse. He and Grandma got interned by the Japanese after they took over Shanghai. After more than a year in a virtual prison camp they were exchanged and evacuated to Los Angeles, where they stayed until they could go back to Shanghai at the end of the war."

"He was still working for the same company, but he now also did some work for the American Secret Service. And he got involved with people that he had met in the internment camp a few years before. Some very bad people. He never told me about the last year in Shanghai, in 1949, when the communists were coming and the country slowly slid into chaos, but I knew that something horrible must have happened just before they had to leave. I often asked about those times, but he always said he would tell me some other time."

DEAN HELD HIS breath. He had only clearly seen one photo from that camera, but it was obvious that Karen's grandfather was the man behind the camera. Had he murdered somebody? Dean did not want to interrupt her, so he just kept quiet and waited for her to continue.

"Now last month my grandfather died. Grandma Estelle, his wife, wanted to move in with my parents since she didn't want to live alone. She is now already eighty-eight years old and can't walk that well anymore. She asked us to take care of their apartment and after cleaning out everything we wanted to keep, we held a big yard sale and a kid in the neighborhood bought this camera and then resold it on eBay."

She had been staring at the camera while she was talking and now she suddenly looked up and into his eyes. Dean was taken aback by her intensity.

"So why do you want the camera back?" He asked.

"There is something else. About a week ago I finally found enough courage to open this letter. My grandfather's letter. He had written a letter to me several months ago when he fell ill and he had told me not to open it until later. That's what he said — 'until later'."

She focused her attention back at the camera.

"In this letter he talked about what had happened in those last days in Shanghai, and that this camera..." She took the camera from the table and held it up on the palm of her right hand.

"*This* camera!"

She now held the heavy camera with both hands and turned it around and around while looking back at Dean. "That this camera contains a film with evidence of a murder..." she continued almost inaudibly "...and a treasure map."

2

DEAN'S THOUGHTS HAD been ahead "Listen, about the film. I have already... What?"

He stared at her, his mouth open. Karen almost had to laugh at his incredulous expression.

"Did... did you say 'treasure map'?"

This had been too much. He had seen a photo of a murdered man, had been threatened and followed by a group of mysterious men - who actually had also offered him a lot of money, now that he thought of it. And then to top it all off he was sitting in a café with an attractive stranger who told him stories about *treasure maps?*

KAREN WAS STILL watching him bemusedly. She had anticipated this kind of reaction, had planned for it, had been waiting for it. But one thing had been wrong. She frowned.

"Interesting. You don't seem to mind about the murder."

He shrugged "Oh, I do mind. It's just... I have already seen the picture."

Now it was on her to stare at him. Her eyes became big. "You... what? When? How is that possible?"

"When you called. I was in my dark room developing the film from your granddad's camera and I was just done printing the first picture when the phone rang. It was quite a shock, I can tell you that. Usually when I find film in some old camera it is just a bunch of pictures of smiling kids."

"I want to see the pictures! Do you have them with you?"

"No. As I've said, only one of them is printed. The film is in my office." He remembered what she had said before. "So... what was that about *treasure?*"

KAREN LOOKED AT him, judging him. Dean was a few inches taller than her, had a long face that invited smiles, light brown hair that was thinning over his forehead. His skin was lightly tanned and gave the appearance of somebody who spent a lot of time outdoors without trying too hard to either stay out of the sun or get a serious tan. The most attractive feature in his face were the very light gray eyes that seemed to see everything, very much like the eyes of a cat.

Could she trust this stranger? She probably had already said too much anyway and she couldn't very well stop him from looking at the pictures. She had no idea what the pictures actually showed other than the hints from her granddad's letter. At that moment, Karen wanted to see those pictures more than anything else.

Decision time.

"Maybe we can work together. You have the pictures, I have the letter." She smiled at him with her head leaning to one side.

"Maybe." He smiled back at her. "Now will you tell me about the treasure, or not?"

"Not here." She looked around. They were alone in the café, only the woman behind the counter could possible hear what they were talking about, but she seemed to be deep into a book she was reading.

But Dean had another thought altogether. "Uhm... there is actually something else we have to talk about. Does anybody else know about this?"

Karen looked surprised. "I guess my grandmother knows. But she never told anybody. Never... why?"

"Somebody else knows. When I came out of my office tonight, there were three men in the parking lot who tried to get the camera from me. They knew my name, where I am and that I had bought this camera. Three more were waiting in front of my apartment. In fact, I don't know where to go tonight."

"What do you mean? They were *waiting* for you? I can't imagine who would possibly know about this."

"I have no idea. The three guys in front of the office new my name and at least one of them had a gun."

"What?" She looked at him in shock.

Dean had to get a better picture of what really was going on. "I would like to read the letter, if you don't mind."

"I have the letter upstairs in my room. I'll go and..." Karen started to get up.

"Wait. Karen, I have to ask you a favor. Tomorrow morning we can try and get into my office. But until then it seems I need a place to hide. Those guys looking for me really looked like they mean business. Is there a second bed in your room?" Dean hoped it didn't sound like an especially spectacular come-on.

Karen was half-standing. Now she stood up and very deliberately unhooked her handbag from the back of the chair. She looked at him. "Sure. It's a twin. Let's go."

Dean grabbed the camera from the table, nodded at the woman behind the counter who gave him a suggestive smile and actually winked at him. He shrugged, smiled and followed Karen to the elevators.

3

Dear Karen,

I'm writing this letter knowing that I will not be there when you read it. I had a long life and there is no mystery in dying for me. Many of my close friends have gone before me and I look forward to meeting them again. I will miss my dear Estelle. Please take good care of her.

I had a good life, a life to be proud of. With one exception.

You have often asked me about our final days in Shanghai, and I owe you an answer. Estelle could tell you some of this, but I know that she does not have the heart to ever talk about it.

During my time with BritOil in Shanghai, I came into contact with several American intelligence service agents, some of whom had very good contacts with the Chinese police and Chiang Kaishek's secret service.

In 1949, just before the Communists arrived in Shanghai, boats were leaving day and night to bring Chinese Nationalists and everything they owned to the island of Taiwan. Billions of dollars worth of gold,

jewelry and artworks was shipped out of
Shanghai. One of my intelligence contacts,
Peter Koshitzky, an American, asked me if I
could organize several trucks and drivers
from the BritOil compound for some overtime
work for a Nationalist friend of his. He
said that we would not regret doing this,
that there was good money to be made if we
would help his friend.

Well, I was still young and stupid, even
with Estelle trying her hardest to transform
me into a thinking adult. So I agreed, and
the next night we took three trucks to
Peter's friend's country villa out on the
road to Soochow. We spent several hours
loading the trucks with everything this man
owned. There were paintings and sculptures,
a lot of ancient Chinese art, suitcases full
of US dollars and also quite a number of
boxes filled with gold bars.

It was maybe three o'clock in the morning
when we drove them straight down through the
middle of Shanghai to the docks at the Bund.
Peter had organized some armed guards, but
what he didn't know was that we were both
just pawns in a chess game played by
Shanghai's mighty.

Things went bad before we made it to the
waterfront. The guards, as it turned out,
had been instructed by their real employer
to divert the trucks down to Soochow Creek,
not far from the Compton House Hotel. They
were to kill us all, Peter, me and the drivers. Peter realized at the last moment what
was going on and we both jumped off the
truck, off a bridge and into a boat that was
going upstream on Soochow Creek. Shots were
fired, but they all missed.

The drivers were not so lucky. My greed
had killed three good men. The next day, I

brought my camera to Soochow Creek to where
the empty trucks had been found so that I
could take pictures for the BritOil lawyers.
A runner found me there and gave me a message from Peter. I was to come to the
Compton House Hotel, room 517, under strict
secrecy.

When I went there, I found Peter dead. He
had been stabbed. I searched the room and I
suddenly knew where the gold had gone. I
still carried the camera, and I started doc-
umenting what had happened. I still don't
know why I did that. As if losing a good
friend and getting four people killed was
not enough. I brought danger onto myself and
my family, even until today, more than fifty
years later. For that I apologize.

Now this is important. I did some research
into this later, when the Communists had
made access to Shanghai impossible. I
believe that Peter's friend thinks that we
ran away with his treasure and this man is
still alive in Hong Kong. His name is Martin
Yau. He is a powerful man and very dangerous.

Before I realized what kind of a man this
Mr. Yau is, I had tried to contact him and
explain to him what had happened. This was
while we were still in Seattle, directly
after we made it back to the States in late
1949. This man immediately started to
threaten me in the worst possible manner and
I broke off all contact. I was afraid I had
already said too much.

Estelle and I had already prepared for our
move to Chicago and so I tried my best to
disguise our tracks as we left Seattle.
Martin Yau may have figured out that we left
for the mid-west, but it seems he never
found us again.

From what I was able to research, nobody
ever found the treasure, either. Mr. Yau's
opponents in Shanghai probably had to leave
only days later for Taiwan, or maybe they
stayed behind and got into trouble with the
communists.

I never developed the film, in fact, I
never even took it out of the camera. It's
in the Kodak Medalist on the top of the
bookshelf in the study. This film is like a
treasure map, but this treasure already cost
the lives of many men.

It is haunted gold. I'm not joking when I
say that.

My dear Karen, please be careful with this
knowledge. I may still decide to burn this
letter, but if you read this then it is up
to you to decide what to do.

I still always call you my little girl,
and I hope you forgive this old man, because
he knows better. You are a big girl now.

Love,

Your Granddad

4

DEAN WOKE UP with a start. It took him a moment to remember that he was staying at the downtown Hilton in his own hometown. He had been traveling extensively for his photo assignments, but he could never get used to staying in a hotel in San Francisco.

"Good morning. Do you always wake up like that?"

Dean looked over his shoulder. Karen had already showered and dressed and was using the smoothed out surface of her bed to spread out a newspaper. On her knee she was balancing a steaming cup of coffee from the little kitchenette. She smiled at him.

"Good morning. No... it's just... for one moment I thought it was all just a very strange dream."

"Want some coffee?" She didn't wait for an answer, got up and poured a cup of coffee at the kitchenette counter. She walked over and gave him the cup.

"Thanks." After a sip from the hot coffee, Dean's brain finally accepted this new reality he was living in.

"Karen, we'll have to get the film out of my office. I'd say we drive down there and see if I still have fans waiting for my appearance."

"Sure. But then what? Do you want to go off hunting for treasure?" She sat down next to him on the bed.

He turned around to face her, the light from the window turning his gray eyes almost white. "That's a possibility." Dean shrugged. "I mean, what else can we do? Somebody else knows about the gold. They are after me. If they figure out that you have this letter, I guess we are both going to be prime targets. And we can't really go to the police with such a story – a fifty-five year old murder in Shanghai and a treasure map on a handful of old photos? They'd be less than impressed."

"YEP, THERE'S THE Blue Men Group..."

Dean's Honda Civic rolled past his office on Third Street. His and Karen's heads were slowly swiveling and their eyes were trained on the black BMW parked in Dean's usual spot. One man was sitting in the driver's seat, while two more in sharp-looking dark blue suits were leaning against the back fender, smoking.

"I don't believe this! That can't be the same guys from last night. How many of them are there?"

Karen was looking over her shoulder at the men. "Stop at the next corner."

Dean rolled to a stop. "You have an idea?"

"Yeah. Whatever happens, don't worry. I'll be OK – I've been doing kick-boxing since I was sixteen." She opened the door and flashed a smile at him.

"What? Hey! You can't just walk up to them!"

"Give me the key to the office." She was out on the sidewalk leaning back into the car, holding out her hand.

"Here." He pulled the key off his keyring and gave it to her. "It's suite 307. The film is in the darkroom on the workbench. Oh – and bring my travel bag along."

"Pick me up in front of the doors in 30 minutes." She pushed the door shut and walked back towards the elevated highway. Under the highway she crossed 3rd Street, passing a crew of workers that were digging a long narrow ditch along the sidewalk on the other side.

She was swinging her hips a little bit more than usual and one of the workers gave her a catcall.

DEAN HAD TO look over his left shoulder and across the street, and he could easily see the three goons and their BMW, just around the corner of the entrance to the office.

Karen walked towards the building when she saw that the two smokers in the blue suits had noticed her. Not just noticed, actually. They had *recognized* her! One of them said something in Chinese and elbowed the other one in the ribs. They both stood up straight, dropped their cigarettes and walked towards the sidewalk.

"Miss Chadbourne?" They knew her name! "Could we talk to you please?"

Karen changed direction and walked straight up to them. One of the men took a step back. Karen grabbed his arm and pulled him forcefully towards her and into the other men. They all bumped together.

"Miss Chadbourne? What..."

She turned her head so that the workers would hear her. "Help! What are you doing! Help! Somebody please help!" She screamed at the top of her lungs. At the same time she kicked one man's shin with the tip of her boot and then rammed the heel into a foot under hers.

The construction workers looked up and saw two men holding on to a screaming woman. Three of them put down their tools and started jogging towards the scene.

The BMW's engine revved up and shot out of the parking spot, stopping right next to Karen and the two men. Karen let go of the men, pushed them away and turned around to deliver a good kick. The heavier of the two men lost balance and screamed something in Chinese. He tried to open the back door of the car.

Karen kicked the guy still upright while behind her the workers were coming up with their fists swinging.

Two of the BMW's doors flew open and the two men dived in. The car was moving already with the doors open, flying out into traffic on 3rd Street. Karen could hear somebody screaming furiously in the car. She turned around, with tires squealing behind her.

"Oh, thank you! Thank you so much for saving me!" She hugged the first of the workers coming up behind her. She put some more trembling into her voice. "I don't know what I would have done without you." That at least was true.

ONLY MINUTES LATER - after leaving a few lipstick smudges on the surprised worker's cheeks - Karen was opening the door to Suite 307. It was a small office, smaller than hers in Chicago, but very neat and practical. She liked Dean's taste in furniture and wouldn't have minded to have the same Scandinavian desk he had. She'd have to ask where he bought this stuff.

She picked the snaking film from the workbench and rolled it between her index finger and thumb. She also grabbed the one print still hanging on the dryer line.

When she finally looked at the letter-sized print, it was a shock. Up to now her Grandfather's stories had been just that — stories of an old men. But this picture changed how she thought of him. He had taken this picture of a murdered friend. He had stood in that hotel room. He had been *there*.

5

DEAN WAS LOOKING at her in a different way when he picked her up at the door of his office building. She threw his travel bag into the back of the car and dropped herself into the passenger seat, pulled the door shut and leaned back heavily with a big sigh. Her face was flushed.

"That was amazing!" He was laughing "I'm glad you are on my team. You totally kicked their ass."

She smiled at that. Yeah, it head been good to let go. She had been frustrated and stressed out for several weeks now, and this had been a pretty good excuse to blow off some steam.

She looked out the window at a foggy and windy San Francisco morning. "Where are we going?"

He already had a destination in mind. "Duboce Park, not far from here. There is a public photo center with a darkroom where we can print the rest of the pictures."

ONLY A FEW minutes later they arrived at the Park and it was easy to find parking right at the Photo Center since it was mid-day Tuesday. It was a bigger place than Karen had expected, with a huge darkroom with more than two dozen workstations. The place was very quiet, probably because it was the middle of the week, and Dean had no problem setting up everything to get the rest of the pictures printed.

She enjoyed watching Dean work in the darkroom. His movements were very efficient and he was very much on top of the whole process. It was almost magical how the images started to appear in the developer fluid. A white sheet of paper suddenly transformed itself into a photo. She was almost disappointed that they had only this one roll of photos to print.

ONCE THEY HAD good prints of the other seven photos on the roll, they went down the street to a small café, picked up some coffee and sandwiches and went into the park for an impromptu picnic. The fog had receded enough towards the ocean to allow the sun to warm the park. It was still a little on the cool side, but just about as warm as a day in mid-July in San Francisco ever got.

KAREN LEANED BACK on the park bench, letting the sun and the wind gently tickle her skin. She smiled, enjoying the moment. She had finally seen the pictures, and even their gruesome subjects couldn't dampen her mood.

"Dean?"

"Hmm?" He was also leaning back, but his head was turned and he was watching her intently. She looked relaxed, and her mood gave her face some kind of special glow. His inner photographer wanted to take her picture.

"I've seen the pictures now, but I don't understand what my granddad meant when he called them a treasure map."

He kept on watching her. "It's clear from his letter that he thinks that the pictures point at a place where the gold was hidden. Since most of the pictures are from the hotel room where Mr. Koshitzky was murdered, the boxes must have been either hidden in the hotel or there is something in the room that would tell us where everything went. I can't really imagine that the gold was hidden in the hotel and stayed there for the last fifty-five years. I've actually been to Shanghai, and -"

She turned around and looked at him "Really? You were there on vacation?"

"No, I've been there on assignment for a travel website that closed down a few years ago. That was too bad because they had oodles of venture capital and they sent me all over the place on a very lavish budget."

She laughed. "Another San Francisco dot-com story. Everybody who came back to Chicago after the boom had the same stories – but nobody seemed to have any money left." She turned her face back into the sun.

"YEAH, THIS WAS one of those companies." He smiled thinking about the boom. "Crazy times... Anyway, they sent me to China for two months and I spent several weeks walking up and down the Shanghai waterfront – the locals still call it the Bund, like the British did. I took pictures of all the old buildings there, and some of them look remarkably untouched. Especially the Suzhou Hotel – that's the current name of the old Compton House, looks like it hasn't seen much of a renovation since the early nineteen hundreds. But still... fifty five years is a long time for crates full of gold and jewelry to sit in a corner of a working hotel."

He yawned. "We can go over to Market Street and check some facts in one of the Internet cafés there. I'd like to google around a bit to see if anybody ever wrote about a pile of gold being found in Shanghai."

"Yes, we have to do some more research. But I'm sure that the gold has never been found." Karen stretched her arms behind her head.

HE LOOKED AT her in surprise. "Oh – of course! You are right. The guys in the blue suits. Somebody is spending a lot of money to get their hands on the camera..." He sighed. "I wish I would know how they found me. And how they even knew that the camera exists!"

"Yeah, I don't understand that part at all. They know my name. They know your name and where to find you. They know that you have the camera and they expect to find something on that camera..."

Dean looked back at her. "So... who knows about all this?"

Karen ticked off three fingers. "Me. You. Grandma Estelle."

"Who knows about your Grandfather's story?"

Again she counted with her fingers "Me. You. Maybe Grandma. Possibly Martin Yau."

They looked at each other. Dean nodded. "One of the men in blue spoke British English. Many people from Hong Kong do."

"Do you think this Mr. Yau was watching me?"

"It would fit. Your grandfather said in his letter that he suspected that Mr. Yau knows what area your family moved to. Maybe he had somebody routinely scanning the Chicago area newspapers for your grandfather's name. If he saw the obituary he could have hired a detective to find you. He may still be very upset about losing those boxes."

She gave a dry laugh. "So it seems."

THEY WERE IN a small internet café on Market Street near San Francisco's Castro district. Men were walking past the window, hand in hand, while vintage street cars in colorful coats of paint rumbled down the street.

Dean clicked the 'Search' button. He was not very hopeful that anything useful would come up, but one never knows. It would be embarrassing to find out later that they could as well have just typed it into Google.

He scrolled through several pages of search results, but nothing seemed to fit. There were travel sites, lots of information about Shanghai's colorful history... but it seemed nobody had discovered a secret cache of gold in the neighborhood of the Compton House. At least not recently.

Karen tapped his shoulder. "Check this out!" She pointed at her screen.

A long list of articles in Hong Kong newspapers all the way from the 1950s and 60s up to just a week before. All of them discussing Martin Yau's empire of casinos in Macao, his nightclubs in Kowloon, his connections with banking, real estate, prostitution, smuggling, gambling, his dealings with corrupt police officials in at least five Asian countries, his use of violent force against foes and investigators and also his generous donations to museums, orphanages, hospitals and kindergartens.

"Oh... he's quite the renaissance man of crime, isn't he?" Dean kept on scanning down the line of lurid articles. "Well, it explains why your granddad was worried about Mr. Yau. And we should be, too."

Karen was jotting down notes about Martin Yau's career. "Our problem seems to be that Yau thinks we know what is going on. Especially now that we've been running from his men, I'm sure he is convinced that we know where the gold is. Even if we hand over the film and the letter now, there's a chance we still end up with a bullet in the head. He wouldn't have survived for so long if he would be in the habit of leaving witnesses behind."

"So going to the police is now definitely out. They still would see no reason to protect us, but it sure would help Yau to find us." Dean started going through his backpack and he took the folder with the photos out.

HE PUT THE photos down between the two computers they were using, one after another. He looked at each of the pictures again, hoping that different light would reveal something he had missed before. Eight photos, eight clues.

The pictures touched him somehow deep inside. He had goosebumps on his arms.

Dean turned to her, one hand resting on the photos, the other now holding her shoulder. "Karen. I think we will have to go to Shanghai. As long as we are here, we are stuck with Yau's men. We don't have any evidence whatsoever to impress the police with, so there is no protection."

"How would finding the gold help us?" Her eyes became wide. "I mean, do you want to go find the gold and hand it over to Yau?"

"I don't know. It doesn't sound like much of a plan, does it? I just have this feeling that everything is drawing us to Shanghai. We will have to solve a fifty-nine year old crime, find hidden treasure and then make peace with an octogenarian crime lord."

She was laughing, her left hand holding onto his on her right shoulder. "Not much of a plan? That sounds very much like a dot-com business plan to me. You've been in San Francisco for far too long."

Their eyes had locked. Dean enjoyed the warmth of her hand on his, the movement of her shoulder against his arm.

They both leaned toward each other and kissed.

6

Photo #1

Three trucks on the side of a dirt road,
with a river to their right. Further down a
massive steel bridge is crossing the river,
boats of all sizes and types are on the
river and tied to its shores. The flatbeds
of the trucks are empty with the exception
of some ropes and blankets.

Two dead men are lying on the road next to
the last truck, the arms of another body are
visible through the open driver door of the
first truck.

Many people from the neighborhood and from
the boats tied to the shore have the trucks
surrounded and are watching as two Shanghai
police inspectors carefully pull papers out
of the breast pockets of the dead men.

7

THE CATHAY PACIFIC Airbus A340 took off and rumbled into a foggy sky. After only a few seconds the plane punched through the marine layer and glorious sunshine turned the huge aircraft into a silver and green jewel.

Dean could see some of the tall office towers in downtown San Francisco peeking through the fog, before the Airbus banked hard and all he could see was dark blue sky.

They were on their way to Hong Kong. It had only taken one afternoon and evening to prepare for the trip. Both he and Karen had already been living out of suitcases, and he only had to buy a few new things to replace his dirty laundry.

They had checked one more time the previous evening, but there were still some of Yau's men waiting for him in front of his apartment on California Street. So they had stayed one more night in Karen's room in the Hilton, sleeping in separate beds, pretending that the kiss in the café had just been some sort of accident.

Dean looked at Karen in the seat next to him. She was already sleeping with her head rolling to the left and right, in sync with the gentle motion of the aircraft.

He leaned back and looked out the window at an ocean of clouds that from this vantage point looked as solid as icebergs.

LAST NIGHT THEY had dinner at a small Burmese place on Clement Street that was one of Dean's favorite restaurants. The food was cheap and good and invited conversation. They had talked about each other's jobs and Dean was surprised to learn that the woman he had seen kick the butts of a pair of Triad gangsters was an accountant and professional organizer. She worked independently as a contractor and that had allowed her to drop everything and go on this chase for the camera and the treasure map it contained.

After dinner they had started to plan for a trip to Shanghai, but it became clear that they had to go to Hong Kong first, since that was the only place were Karen could get a tourist visa for China overnight. They were lucky that the flight had not been booked out.

He kept on staring out the window, free-associating all the things that had happened over the last 48 hours. He had the feeling that the time on this plane may be their last chance to relax and recharge their batteries. Dean's eyes became heavy and he started to slumber with his forehead against the window.

KAREN WOKE UP later during the flight, covered with a blanket that she couldn't remember. She was disoriented, and it took her a few moments before she remembered where she was going. Hong Kong!

This was exciting. It was her first trip to Asia and after what had happened to her life over the last week, she was looking forward to the adventure of it all. At the same time she was very apprehensive about their chances of escaping the grip of Martin Yau. He didn't seem to have any problems finding them in San Francisco, and he had the means to send his people after them anywhere on the planet.

She leaned back and considered her situation. It was almost as if her grandfather had placed a spell on her with his letter. She still remembered reading it in her office, in a silence only broken by the steady patter of rain on the windows. Chicago's skyline had been blurry with rain and tears.

Then figuring out where the camera had gone and her trip to San Francisco... and now on to Hong Kong. It had been so impulsive, so not like her. What had made her do all of these things?

Karen looked at Dean, peacefully sleeping next to her in the window seat. He was not really her usual type of man, but something about him had caught her attention. He was good humored and calm and he had a good head for thinking problems through. And he stuck with her in something that wasn't necessarily his problem. He could have probably tried to make a deal with Yau and throw her to the wolves, but it seems that this had never even crossed Dean's mind. He was a straight shooter who did what he said.

She liked that.

LATER DURING THE flight, about two hours out from Hong Kong they were served an early dinner. The flight attendant stopped her cart next to their row and the sound woke Dean with a start.

"You do wake up like that a lot, don't you?" Karen laughed.

Dean rubbed his eyes and yawned. "It's a new habit. Too much excitement, I guess."

They both went trough the gymnastics of eating a meal without moving their elbows. Dean was flying a lot, but he had still to encounter the same type of in-flight meal packaging twice. This time, everything was tightly wrapped in some metal-plastic compound that seemed to be able to withstand a nuclear blast. He had already managed to spill gravy on his shirt and he was going to skip the pudding since it looked as if it was not meant to be opened anyway.

Karen was nibbling on a tiny piece of cake. "So... did you say last night you have a friend in Shanghai?"

"Yeah. His name is Mike and he's working there for DynaRola. He is installing cell phone towers all over the Shanghai area and he's earning a mint. The company is actually paying for his apartment. Makes me wish I would have finished my engineering degree." He pushed the tray away and leaned back. "Mike is a really nice guy. I had known him through a friend when he still lived in San Francisco, but we became really close when I was in Shanghai on assignment. He knows that city like the back of his hand, especially all the places where you can get a drink."

"Do you think he can help us?"

"I hope so. I'll try and call him when we are in Hong Kong..."

The flight attendants started picking up the trays and the Fasten Seatbelt light came on. They were descending into Hong Kong.

8

Photo #2

A steel bridge arches out of the frame to
the right. There is a lot of foot traffic,
horse-drawn carriages and 1940s-style cars
are crossing the bridge.

On the other side of the street to the
left of the picture is an imposing building,
six floors of stone masonry with a little
tower in the corner. The stone walls are
dark with light gray, almost white accents
for window arches and corner stones.

Along the front of the building several
cars are parked near the entrance. The roof
over the entrance has a sign along its side,
"Compton House".

9

WELCOME TO HONG KONG
SPECIAL ADMINISTRATIVE REGION

"NICE GREETING." KAREN walked under the sign and into the arrivals hall of the new Hong Kong airport. "Wow! This airport is huge!"

The arrivals area was bustling with people. It was the focal point for international travelers from all over Asia and Karen was now slowly turning on her heels, taking it all in. She had her one bag hanging on a shoulder strap, her purse on her other shoulder. Her arms were crossed in front of her and her hands were holding onto the straps of her bags. She was slowly spinning around and around in amazement.

Dean stood next to Karen, watching her. She looked as happy as he had ever seen her. This trip would be fun. He always enjoyed playing the guide to friends on trips, showing them the world and rediscovering with them how amazing this planet really was.

She stopped turning, facing Dean. Her face was one big smile. "OK, so what now?"

"I guess we get you out of this airport and into Hong Kong proper. There is a direct train into town from over there."

THE TRAIN TOOK them into town in less than half an hour. They got off in Kowloon and took a taxi to the Salisbury Hotel.

They opened the doors of the taxi and the humid heat hit them in full force for the first time since they had arrived. Karen gasped. "Man! This is nasty. It's like walking into a sauna. Is it always like this?"

Dean nodded. "Pretty much all summer. At least today it doesn't smell like the inside of a running shoe. Shanghai will be a little bit better, but not by much. Here's our hotel. I had no chance to book ahead, but this is the place I wanted to check first. It's my favorite place in town."

"Dean! This is a YMCA?"

He laughed. "Not your usual YMCA, trust me. This place is at least as good as the Hilton we just stayed at back in San Francisco."

THEY WERE LUCKY and got one of the very reasonable suites that this YMCA featured, on the tenth floor with harbor view. When Dean unlocked the door, Karen walked in and just stopped. One corner of the room was a floor to ceiling window with a perfect view of the harbor. The hotel was situated close to the tip of Kowloon, across from the island of Hong Kong and separated by the busiest piece of watery real estate on the planet. The harbor was crammed with boats of all sizes, the distinctive green and white ferries, container ships, yachts, and the odd military vessel.

It was turning dark and Hong Kong's skyscraper-encrusted waterfront was aglow in a million lights.

Karen turned around, dropped her bag and hugged Dean. He kicked the door behind him into its lock. They stood there for a moment, only lit by the lights of Hong Kong behind her, and then they kissed, more deliberate this time than in San Francisco.

Later that night after a dinner in a small Indian restaurant in one of the colorful side streets of Kowloon they were back in their suite, naked, holding each other in the sweet afterglow of sex. They fell asleep in an embrace so tight that they could as well have been one.

10

Photo #3

The open window overlooks a busy river
scene from several floors up. A smaller
creek on the right empties into a large
river that is lined by tall buildings. The
small river is being crossed by a long metal
girder bridge.

There are ocean liners and large
freighters on the bigger river, surrounded
by many small watercrafts. The smaller boats
spill in and out of the waterway passing
under the bridge.

A rough rope is coiled into a neat pile on
the floor under the window sill, surrounded
by several shorter pieces of thin rope that
were carelessly tossed aside.

11

KAREN WOKE UP, turned around, expecting to see Dean. His side of the bed was empty and instead she was treated to a panoramic view of Hong Kong island in the morning sun. She rested her head on her arms and enjoyed the view, a smile on her face when she remembered last night. From the living room she could now hear Dean's voice. He was on the phone with what had to be his friend Mike in Shanghai.

"...Yeah, we will be in Shanghai in a day or two..."

"...really? Are you sure that's OK? That's great then..."

"...no, I can't really tell you that on the phone. You'd think I'd gone crazy anyway..."

Karen heard him laughing. "Sure you do. Well, anyway, I'll call you when we are in Shanghai... Hm? ... Yep. Probably Saturday. See you then!"

She turned her head just in time to see him come into the bedroom, stark naked. She liked what she saw.

"Hello stranger."

"Good morning. I hope I didn't wake you up."

"No, not at all. Come here!" She pulled the cover aside.

He lunged under the cover and they hugged. His skin was cold and gave her goosebumps. He kissed her gently and pulled the cover back up. Soon they were both getting warm again.

LATER THAT MORNING they had breakfast in a small and bustling cafeteria on the ground floor of the hotel and were planning what had to be done.

"First, we have to get you set up with a visa for China. We'll drop your passport off for the night and should have the visa in the morning. Then the flight... there's a travel agent across the street in the mall above the ferry terminal – at least there was one two years ago. I hope we can get an early flight on Saturday morning to Shanghai."

"And tomorrow?"

"I have no idea. I don't have any contacts in town, so there is not much we can do about Martin Yau. I guess we are going to play tourists for a day."

Karen liked the sound of this. She felt like she was slowly coming out of a month-long nightmare. It would be nice to forget about everything for a little while.

Dean looked up from his omelet. "Oh – when I talked to Mike, he said we could stay in his place. His apartment has a guest room that he doesn't use and he'd be happy to have us over. If you don't mind, that is."

She enjoyed looking into his open, honest face and she found she really liked his light gray eyes. "Uhh... what?" It was like soap bubbles were exploding over her head. "Oh. Yes, no problem. I hope he's ok with us staying for a while, though. Who knows how long it will take to figure out what my granddad's pictures actually mean."

"Good point. But Mike and his girlfriend are the kind of people who enjoy company. They... like to perform." Karen looked at him puzzled. "No! Not like that. It's just that they behave like they are channeling one of those large Italian families where everything turns into an operatic performance. Lot's of shouting and hand-waving and hugging."

Karen had to laugh at the image he was conjuring up in her mind. "So they are Italian?"

"No, he's Japanese American and she is Chinese. Her name is Jia."

Now Karen was really laughing. So much for preconceptions. "I can't wait. They sound like fun people to hang out with."

"That's for sure."

"Oh – Dean, another thing. It should be possible to get some good books about the history of Shanghai here in Hong Kong. Is there a book shop around here?"

Dean was intrigued. "Good idea! Yeah, I remember seeing a book shop around the corner towards Nathan Road. There are several good coffee table books with old photographs of Shanghai. We should maybe check those and see if we can find one with pictures of the area around the Compton House during the war years. That may help us to identify where the things in the letter actually happened."

THEY SPENT THE rest of the day organizing their trip to Shanghai. The flight tickets were no problem, Karen's visa was on the way, and they had spent several productive hours looking through travel guides and photo collections of old Shanghai.

In the afternoon the city had become steamy with heat and walking around became a chore. They had retreated to the hotel and now spent some time in the air conditioned pool area with a view of the harbor.

Dean pulled himself out of the pool after a few rounds of lazy breaststroke. He rubbed himself off with a thick white towel and let himself fall into a deck chair next to Karen. She was intently reading a book about Shanghai's history.

"This is a big mess. I mean, have you ever read about what went down in Shanghai in the 1930s and 40s? The city had multiple layers of administration for the different nationalities, had been repeatedly bombed and finally invaded by the Japanese, they frequently had labor unrests, were the birthplace of the Chinese Communist party, there were Czarist refugees fleeing from Russia, Jewish refugees pouring in from all over Europe, spies from all nations, smugglers, pimps, drugs, you name it."

"A great place for somebody like Yau to make a fortune. "

"You bet. Him and everybody else. It must have been an exciting place to live. I had heard so many stories from my granddad, but I had never internalized what an amazing place Shanghai must have been for him. Even through the bombings and the internment by the Japanese... he just loved it."

"And your grandmother?"

"Oh – Estelle liked it there, alright. They were both working for a British oil company and their combined income was quite substantial for the time and the place. They were able to hire a servant for the house and a chauffeur for the weekends. That was way above the class they were both coming from." Karen took a sip from her grapefruit juice.

"And she enjoyed the socializing. She grew up in Chicago in a working class family before she found that job in Shanghai, and that was such a different world. Everything was still very class oriented with a lot of Imperial British decorum. By earning good money and being white, they both automatically belonged to clubs... you know, afternoon teas, and all that stuff."

"It must have been quite a shock to come back to egalitarian 1950s-style living in the United States."

"You bet. They pretty much skipped 50 years in their lifestyle, overnight. By then she was pregnant and my father was born shortly after they settled down back in Chicago."

"So where is the Native American influence coming from? Your mother?" He leaned back and relaxed into the shape of the deck chair.

"Yes. My mother's mother was from the Crow tribe. I never met her, she died shortly after my mother was born. Nobody else in the family looks like they have any Native American roots, but with me it's pretty obvious. I've seen pictures of my grandmother and I look a little bit like her. And you? What kind of a name is Lashure anyway?"

"I'm the only person I know who is third generation Bay Area. Both my parents and all my grandparents were born in the area between San Francisco and Monterey. My great-grandfather came to California from somewhere in Wisconsin and I think there's more of the old family over there. The rest of my family tree consists of lucky earthquake survivors and unlucky gold diggers."

She laughed. "You seem to have been traveling a lot?"

"Yeah. I actually lived with my parents in London from when I was six to about sixteen. I went to an American school there, so I never had much chance to make friends with the locals. But it was a good school and the US government paid for it, so that was not so bad."

"Why London?"

"My dad was an electrical engineer and he worked for NASA during the moon shots. They had sent him to London to live there, but he worked all over western Europe for a few weeks at a time. He was maintaining some of the antennas that NASA was using to stay in contact with the astronauts on the moon."

"Oh wow."

"Yeah, I thought my dad was the coolest dad ever – he even met a few astronauts and he brought me autographed photos and mission patches from them. And the traveling was cool, too. He had to go to North Africa a few times and once towards the end of his job there he took me along on a trip into the Moroccan interior."

"But you never finished your engineering degree?"

"No. I honestly wanted to do what my dad did. But by that time the space race was over and NASA was just a bunch of bureaucrats inventing new ways not to go to space... And I discovered photography. I loved it! So I dropped out of school and started my own business as a photographer."

"Was you father disappointed about that?"

"Maybe. I guess so. But he never let on. He actually supported my decision to drop out of school against my mom. He always said that if I do what I love to do I would be doing a great job and having fun doing so. And I guess he was right about that one."

12

Photo #4

The fireplace is very big, set in white
bricks against the dark wood paneling of the
walls. It is almost six feet wide and five
feet tall. Intricate ironworks surround the
fire pit, but the front piece has been taken
out and moved to the side. Ashes are
spilling out of the fire pit.

Two heavy armchairs upholstered in black
leather face the fireplace from about nine
feet away, with a little side table between
them. The side table seems to have recently
lost a leg and it is leaning against one of
the armchairs.

13

IT WAS STILL relatively early in the morning as their little boat chugged along the waterways of Aberdeen harbor on the ocean-facing side of Hong Kong island. The air was fresh and the smell from the water had not taken over yet, but the sun was already high and did its best to turn the harbor into a sauna by noon.

Karen looked back up along the emerald green forests of Hong Kong island. Everywhere in the hills she could see the houses of the rich in splendid isolation, untouchable and decadent for a overcrowded city like this.

"One of these villas is maybe Yau's!" She turned around to Dean who was leaning back on one of the benches, facing the sun with closed eyes. Behind him, the owner of the boat was weaving the boat through dense traffic with elegant swinging motions of the outboard motor.

"Hmmm?" He opened his eyes and simply smiled at her. She bent down and lightly kissed him on his sun-warmed lips.

"Listen to me!" She smiled and stared into his clear, gray eyes. "That's men in a nutshell... got a new girlfriend and two days later you don't even listen to her anymore." She pouted at him. He moved forward and quickly kissed her back.

Dean turned and looked up at Hong Kong island, using his arm to provide shadow over his eyes. "You are right, one of those villas could be Yau's." He looked back at Karen.

"Which makes me wonder about why he is coming after us. I mean, he is stinking rich, for god's sake." He shook his head.

Karen shrugged. "Maybe it is the artwork he is after. It could be that it has some nostalgic value to him that we will never understand. After all, he was still very young back then and he may have inherited most of that stuff."

She became more serious and, despite the sun, felt a chill descend along her spine. Dean felt her shake in his arm. He turned back to her. "Worried?"

"Afraid." She held onto his arm with both hands. "This is a dangerous man, and we are not even sure why exactly he has sent his men to find us. I have the feeling that we are playing a very dangerous game and we don't even understand all the rules."

Dean nodded. "I know what you mean. The guys in the blue suits scared the hell out of me." He sighed. "And I've been thinking about it quite a bit since then, but I still can't figure out what else we could do. Yau wants the pictures - and even if we prove to him that we have destroyed them, he still knows that we have seen them. We would never be safe."

He kissed her on the forehead and smiled. "We'll figure something out."

THEY BOTH LEANED back and looked at the boats all around them. Aberdeen harbor still had tens of thousands of people living on the water, most of their boats tied together to create swimming villages, with narrow channels for the dense boat traffic to pass through.

They were surrounded by the sights of the daily life of the inhabitants of Aberdeen harbor. Children were playing on the decks, a man was brushing his teeth, an old grandma was cleaning fish.

Dean had turned more serious again. "So why are you really here? I don't think you came along to stay with a dashing, soon-to-be successful photographer, or to hunt for hidden treasure."

Karen looked dreamily out across the scenery of the harbor. She shrugged.

"I think my granddad's stories over the years have hit deeper than I'd realized. He always talked of Shanghai with this special tone in his voice, I could feel that it had been the best time of his life. And then at the end it had been this horrible situation!

He felt responsible for the death of several people and what he had done was endangering his new family. It was like a nightmare that he would never be able to escape from." She looked down.

"So you want to break the curse." He put his arm around her shoulders and pulled her close.

She looked back up at him. "Yes. I'm going to go to Shanghai. I have no idea what I'm doing, but there must be a way to make it better. My granddad did whatever he did, but maybe..." She sighed. "Maybe I can fix it *somehow*. Does that sound very stupid?"

"No. I've heard worse ideas." He flashed a smile at her. "Well, not much worse."

She had to laugh at that.

14

Photo #5

The two armchairs are standing on a lightly patterned oriental rug. The leather back
of one of the armchairs is streaked with
scratches.

Behind one of the chairs is a piece of
carved wood, presumably from the leg of the
side table. Several long dirt stains are
visible on the light color of the carpet,
running all the way from the fireplace to
the chairs, and several dirty boot prints
make a track across the carpet, from between
the chairs towards the position of the photographer.

15

THEY HAD ONLY been able to get tickets to Shanghai with one of the smaller local airlines, but the service on board the ShanghaiTrans Boeing 757 had been courteous and the flight had been on time.

It was a pretty short flight and they were still nibbling on the contents of their packages of "A Chinese Snack", which to all the world looked like roasted peanuts, when the plane started to descend into Shanghai's Pudong International Airport.

Karen was looking forward to Shanghai. She had been listening to stories about that city for all her life, but never had she dared to dream that one day she would visit this faraway place.

Hong Kong had been an eye-opener for her. While she had been traveling to Europe before and considered herself culturally attuned to the realities of living in the 21st century, she had been amazed to see all the different cultural influences at work in Hong Kong.

And while Chicago was not exactly a sleepy hamlet, she had been overwhelmed by the sheer energy of this multicultural tornado. Their "day off" had been well-spent with sight-seeing and boat rides, good food and intriguing glimpses into south-east Asian and Chinese culture.

And now Shanghai. It just sounded so exotic to her ears. She willed the plane forward to arrive even faster.

Then there was of course Dean. She had spent several years without a deep relationship and this was a welcome surprise. Dean was fun to be with and he seemed to genuinely love her. Maybe she had already found some treasure on this trip.

FLYING FROM THE new Hong Kong airport to the Shanghai Pudong airport was like flying from one futuristic construction site to another. Both were still not completely finished, both were huge and both were full of all the shiny 21st century technology that money could buy.

The main attraction of the Pudong Airport was a Maglev Train that zoomed the openmouthed Dean and Karen into the city in less than ten minutes.

They emerged out of the subterranean station into overcast and humid Shanghai. The air enveloped them like a wet blanket and pearls of sweat were appearing on Deans forehead so fast that Karen could watch them grow.

"Wow." Dean pulled his travel bag up on his shoulder and looked around. "That was fast." He took Karen's hand and they stood there for a while, hand-in-hand, taking it all in.

KAREN WAS STUNNED. While the street they were on could well have been somewhere in the States, it was at the same time without doubt China. The subject of her grandfather's tales of a land far, far away. And now she was there. Here. She felt like crying and laughing at the same time.

Dean looked at her. "Are you OK?"

"Yes. It's just... This is Shanghai!" She laughed... and then coughed. "And the air in this place is nasty!"

"Yeah, hasn't changed much since my last time here. It's always like this." He was scanning the street for a sign of Mike.

He had called his friend from the airport and Mike had promised to pick them up at the exit for the maglev trains.

"Ah! There he is!" Dean started waving and walking along the line of taxis.

Now Karen could see him, too. Dean's friend was tall, more then six feet, with thick, unruly black hair that stood up in all directions like little wires. He had a handsome, smiling face with surprisingly thick eyelashes. He was wearing a white shirt and dark jeans and he stood with one foot out of his small red car of unidentifiable heritage, with one arm and leg still inside. He was so big compared to the car, it looked like he was holding it in his hand.

The other door popped open and a beautiful, tall, slender Chinese woman unfolded herself from the tiny car. To Karen's envy she managed to do this gracefully in a super-miniskirt and high heels.

"DEAN! WELCOME BACK!" screamed the woman against the noise in the street. She ran towards Dean and almost toppled him backwards, more jumping at him than hugging him. At the same time Mike came around the car and walked past the spectacle of his girlfriend and Dean and held a hand out for Karen to shake.

"Hi. Welcome to Shanghai. You must be Karen - I've only heard good things about you. I'm Mike Moritaka." He had a winning smile and a warm, solid handshake.

"Karen Chadbourne. Nice to meet you." She couldn't help but look past Mike at his girlfriend who was still hugging Dean.

Mike pointed over his shoulder with his thumb. "And that's Jia, my girlfriend. She's always like that." He said with a happy smile.

JIA HAD UNWRAPPED herself from Dean and came over to Karen and held out a hand. "Hi. I'm Jia. Nice to meet you." Her English had a musical lilt to it.

"Karen. Nice to meet you." Again a good handshake. Jia was even more spectacular close-up. A natural beauty that can not really be defined with only a few words. It was more how she moved and how her face changed with her emotions than just superficial beauty that could be obtained with enough makeup. Right now she displayed a big teethy smile. "You'll have to tell me everything about the two of you. Dean seems to really like you a lot."

This was overheard by Dean who had come up behind. He turned beet-red from ear to ear.

Karen smiled at poor Dean and took Jia's arm as they walked back to the car. "And you will have to tell me all about Dean. You know so much more about him than me, I'm sure."

Mike laughed at that and slapped Dean's shoulder. "Women! Let's get the two of you settled in our place and then you'll have to explain to me where those sudden urges to travel to China come from."

MIKE'S CAR WAS even smaller when seen up close and it took some maneuvering to get the four of them into the seats. Jia and Karen were sitting in the back with her travel bag between them, and Dean sat in the passenger seat with his bag on his knees. Dean was very impressed by the absence of any major instruments on the dashboard, other than a rickety FM radio and a small round speedometer with an unmoving arrow stuck at 80 kilometers per hour. Several big holes indicated the absence of more lavish instrumentation.

Dean smiled his most harmless smile at Mike "Nice car!"

Mike hit him on the shoulder while his head bumped off the roof. "Very funny! I bought this one second hand from a taxi company for a hundred dollars. It may look like shit, but it goes like crazy and fits into any parking spot. Just watch." He hit the gas and catapulted them out of the taxi line and into the massive traffic jam that was Shanghai's daily commute.

"Oh – and I don't care if somebody adds another dent to the collection!"

"So how is business?" Dean looked at Mike.

"Can't complain. Everybody in this town has at least one cell phone. I swear, we've sold more of these things than there are people in the city!" He swerved aggressively to avoid a nasty collision with a bike carrying a brand new washing machine. "Hey! Careful there!" Now their little car was facing oncoming traffic – specifically a large truck bearing down on them. More evasive action and they found themselves back in their own lane between a lumbering, overloaded city bus and about two dozen motor scooters.

Mike seemed to not even notice. "Anyway, so yeah, I'm spending my days on pretty much every roof in town installing cell phone transmitters."

JIA ALREADY HAD some experience with first-time western visitors to her home town, so she didn't even try to make small talk with Karen in the car. She just watched as Karen leaned forward and put her hands on Deans shoulders, massaging them gently, staring out the window with a transfixed gaze of wonder.

Karen couldn't believe how dense the traffic was in this city. Trucks, buses, cars, motorbikes and scooters, bikes, bicycle-rickshaws, porters on foot with goods on bamboo canes – just about everybody and everything was on the road with them. There were so many people in the streets, walking, talking, just sitting in front of houses watching the world go by. Old people playing mahjong on small folding tables under trees, mothers with their children, swarms of schoolchildren in blue-and-white uniforms with bright yellow hats.

A lot of Shanghai's daily life happened on the side of the street. Children were playing at the feet of their grandmothers, housewives were cleaning vegetables or sewing, bikes were repaired, car engines were taken apart. Old men were playing cards, chess and mahjong, or discussing the latest news.

They were passing a small park, really only a few trees with benches, where a group of mobile hairdressers had set up shop, cutting the hair of their customers al fresco with the children of the neighborhood looking on.

Karen turned to Jia with big eyes. "This is amazing. Dean said you are from Shanghai?"

"Yes. I was born not far from here, actually very close to where Mike and me are living now. If we have time, I'll take you to my parents' house sometime. That part of town hasn't changed so much yet – you'll love it."

They were crossing a major road by the looks of it. All the traffic had to go around a massive circle. Jia pointed to her left down the main street. "This is Nanjing Lu, the main street of Shanghai. From here all the way down to the Bund for about three kilometers is the best shopping in China." She flashed her white teeth in a smile. "*Lot's* of shopping."

Karen laughed. She already liked Jia a lot. She had a good spirit.

DEAN HAD BEEN very quiet in the front seat, looking out the window and meditating about what they had to do next. It looked like an almost insurmountable problem. Up to now they had been running on sheer momentum, kicked into motion by the men in the blue suits in San Francisco. Coming all the way to Shanghai now seemed almost ridiculous, with the blue men now being so far away. He would have to talk this through with Mike and see how somebody else would react to this story.

He hoped he wouldn't sound completely paranoid. But then he remembered the first photo he had seen from that roll of film, the last one Karen's granddad had taken with that camera.

The man with the knife in his breast.

16

Photo #6

The carpet is bunched up near the window
and small wood splinters are scattered
around.

To the left, the end of a bed is partially
visible, with the feet of a man in shoes
pointing at the ceiling. The cover of the
bed is smooth, nobody has been sleeping in
the bed last night. Next to the right foot
is a small dark stain on the light-colored
bed cover.

17

MIKE WAS KICKING the door wide open. "Welcome to the Scotland Residence." He had insisted on carrying the two bags for his house guests, and he dropped them now unceremoniously on a sofa in the large living room.

Karen looked around and discovered a picture of dark green highlands shrouded in fog on one wall. "Scotland Residence?"

"That's what they call this building. It's managed by the hotel next door. We even can get room service from over there. A very nice thing if you don't have to pay for it. My employer pays for the apartment and I even have a daily food budget." He gave her a toothy smile.

Dean had visited him in this apartment once before, but Karen was very impressed with the size of the rooms and the style of the furnishing. "Beautiful furniture!"

"Oh no. I didn't buy all this stuff – you should have seen my old apartment back in San Francisco. This apartment comes furnished, courtesy of the Scotland Residence. All I did was stick some pictures on the walls. Here is your room." He opened the door to the generous guest room with a large double bed. The room had it's own little bathroom.

Jia shouted from the kitchen. "Anybody want some drinks?"

"Me!" Mike shouted back. "One Sapporo please!"

Dean smiled at Karen and winked. "A beer for me too, please."

Karen smiled back and shrugged. She raised her voice. "And some water for me. Thank You!" She turned back into the living room, walked across, and looked at the view from the large window. The sixth floor apartment was set back from the street in front of the building, but this window gave a good view of the street scene below.

She looked at the traffic down below and marvelled again at the rich life visible everywhere. A neverending stream of bicycles rolled past the building, hundreds of people busy with their lives.

MIKE SAT DOWN cross-legged in front of the low table in the living room with the sofa on the other side. "OK. And now I want to hear your mysterious story. What brought you to Shanghai?"

Dean and Karen sat down on the sofa. Jia yelled from the kitchen. "Wait! Wait! I want to hear this, too!"

Seconds later she appeared with a tray full of bottles and glasses, put it down on the table and sat close to Mike, her arm around his waist.

Karen told the story of her grandfather, his camera and the letter. She told about tracking down Dean, and finally meeting him in San Francisco.

Dean laid the photos out on the table. And then, to a rapt audience, he told the story of Karen's fight against the blue-suited men. And their plan to find the gold and fight back against Martin Yau.

Mike had his mouth hanging open for the last ten minutes. He drank the last of his beer, looking back and forward between Karen and Dean.

"YOU KNOW THAT you are completely crazy? I am not even going to start about the fact that you both reacted a tad paranoid about those guys in suits. But going on a treasure hunt? In Shanghai? You do realize that we've successfully made it to the 21st century, do you? People don't go treasure hunting anymore."

Dean shrugged. "I wouldn't have been interested if I didn't have that encounter with those guys in the parking lot. They knew everything about me and offered me ten thousand dollars for the camera. Just like that. How else would you explain that? They know that there is something to the story."

"And then there is my granddad's letter." Karen chimed in. "I mean, he was old and everything, but he had his wits together until the very end. And these photos match his story perfectly. Remember, he had never actually seen these pictures." She pointed at the row of pictures on the table.

JIA HAD PICKED up the last picture, the one with the dead man, and walked over to the window to take a closer look.

The picture, printed on a sheet of eight by ten inches seemed to grow in front of her eyes. It was almost like she was falling into the room with the dead man. She rapidly pulled the picture down and away. Her eyes refocused on the street.

A delicate, whispered sound from Jia. "Oh." Her arms dropped to her sides and she let go of the picture. It sailed to the ground in a lazy arc.

"What is it, honey?" Mike looked worried and jumped up.

Jia unsteadily turned away from the window. Her face had become pale and she was leaning against the glass. "I believe them." She reached out for Mike's hand and pulled him closer. With her other hand she pointed over her shoulder. "Look. There are the three men in blue suits."

18

Photo #7

He had been a good-looking man. Even in
death his face was composed, relaxed. He has
a large mustache over full lips, thick,
well-formed eyebrows, strong chin.

He is wearing a dark vest over a white
shirt with a dark tie neatly knotted. The
tie slipped to one side and where it should
be, a large knife, shaped like a hunting
knife, is sticking up to the hilt in the
breast of the man.

The attacker had hit right above the heart
on the left side of the breast, death must
have been instantaneous.

At the edge of the frame the hands of the
man are visible. The palm of his left hand
and the shirt cuff are dirtied with black
dust.

19

"WHAT?" EXCLAIMED DEAN and Karen in unison. They jumped up from the sofa and came to the window at a brisk pace. All four of them looked down at the street in front of the Scotland Residence.

There was a heavy black Volkswagen limousine parked across the street and behind it on the sidewalk stood three men in dark blue suits and sunglasses. Their hair was cropped short and their behavior marked them as being trained to react disciplined, giving them the distinct aura of soldiers or mercenaries.

Their heads turned continually and slowly as they scanned the crowds around them, not particularly paying attention to the building across the street, but at least one of them always seemed to keep an eye on the front entrance.

"Th... that's not possible! Shit!" Dean was flabbergasted. He turned to Karen who was pressing her nose against the window to get a closer look of the men. "How on earth did they follow us? From San Francisco to Hong Kong to Shanghai?"

"It sounds impossible, doesn't it?" Karen said very quietly, her breath creating a foggy circle on the glass.

Mike was holding Jia, who was still a bit rattled, and looked back at them. "OK. That is really impressive. So you didn't make this thing up after all, hm?" He and Jia walked back and dropped heavily onto the sofa.

Dean and Karen at the window looked at each other. "Maybe if we leave now we can avoid dragging Mike and Jia deeper into this mess." Karen said.

"Good point. Hey, Mike! We are lea..."

"No, you are not!" Mike looked back at them. "The Moritakas are not known for abandoning their friends. You are in trouble. You came to our house. We'll help." He looked at Jia next to him. She grabbed his head, pulled him closer and gave him a big sloppy kiss.

"That's my man!" Jia smiled at Karen and Mike.

DEAN PICKED UP the photo that Jia had dropped on the carpet. All of them sat down again, but now with Dean and Karen on the floor.

"Let's go over this one more time. I'd like to hear a few more details, now that I have a bunch of Triad gangsters in front of my house." Mike said.

"Triads? You think so?" Dean didn't like the sound of that at all.

"Yep. Your new friend, whatshisname, Martin... Yau? He's been living it up in Hong Kong, right?" He held up the printout that they had made in the Internet café in San Francisco with the list of newspaper articles about Yau. "Look at this... owns a casino, bribery, shootout at the docks, drugs, prostitution, runs a bunch of night clubs in Kowloon, another shootout, more bribery..." He dropped the paper on top of the photos. "This guy has been involved in organized crime for the last sixty years! He practically *owns* the triads!"

Karen looked at them. "Triads? What are you talking about?"

Mike took another beer from the tray, opened it and leaned back. "Triads are the Hong Kong mafia. Each Triad is essentially a big gang, often run by the most ruthless of the bunch who just couldn't get killed off by any of the other members of the gang. You can assume the older the tougher. Your Mr. Yau is almost ninety years old. And he held a grudge against your grandfather for more than fifty-five years." he took a swig from the bottle. "Oh – and you beat up a couple of his men!" He held the bottle up in salute to Karen.

"Oh." Karen looked like she was about to faint.

DEAN CLEARED HIS throat unsuccessfully, gave up, and drank from his beer. He coughed. "Ugh. Too much dry air in the airplane. So... how on earth did Yau find us here? We had no pre-bookings, Karen didn't call anybody back in Chicago because we thought her phone there might be tapped. I didn't tell anybody about this until I called you from the YMCA in Hong Kong..."

Jia had picked up the printouts and had been browsing through them, stopping from time to time to read something more closely. While the others kept on talking, she got up and woke the laptop on a desk in the corner. The screen came to life and she started typing.

Mike was talking at the table. "I don't know. You sure they didn't just plain tail you all the way to here?"

"I can't imagine. I'd think we would have noticed those guys... they are pretty obvious, aren't they?"

"Or maybe..." Mike's thought was interrupted by Jia who was checking a Chinese-language website.

"Dean, Karen! What flight were you on this morning?"

"ShanghaiTrans flight 712. Why?" Dean had turned around to look at Jia.

"Martin Yau owns ShanghaiTrans." She looked back at them.

"Oh man... we are so fucked!" Dean buried his face in his hands. Karen wrapped her arms around him from behind as she leaned her cheek against his shoulder.

Dean looked up at Jia again. "When we booked the ticket to Shanghai, we must have lit up his computer screen like a Christmas tree. And I guess they just followed us from the airport to your place."

MIKE WAS LEAFING through the photos again. He looked at each one individually. He spoke with a low voice, deep in thought. "Well, well, well. Trucks with gold. Empty trucks. The Compton House. Ropes in a room of the Compton. A dead man."

He looked up at them. "Ladies and Gentleman. I'd like to propose that we go and get the gold. Then at least that old bastard has a real reason to hate us."

"For starters, we can maybe go down to the Bund and take a look at the Compton House – or Suzhou Hotel, as they call it now." Dean looked at them. "We should look at the area and see if it matches the photos. If we assume that somebody robbed three trucks full of valuables and carted everything off to the Compton House, I'd like to see how far they had to bring everything. Boxes of gold would be very heavy. You don't want to go on a hike with something like that."

Mike nodded. "The gang that had organized the robbery must have known what would be on the trucks, they probably had a spy in Yau's household." He drank from his beer. "And getting cheap day laborer to help carry boxes along the waterfront was easy then and is still easy nowadays."

JIA HAD FOLLOWED this discussion and had become more and more restless. "You are always talking about treasure. Would it be that much money?" She shrugged. "I just want to make sure we know what we are fighting for."

Dean looked at her. "Good question. I've actually once taken pictures of gold bars for a jeweler friend of mine back in San

Francisco. There's many different kinds, but from what I remember, I'd expect them to be about two pounds each." He held his hands about one foot apart. "And one box is probably not bigger than this with maybe 20 bars in it. So each bar is about... 32 ounces and – well, who knows the price for gold?"

Karen got up and sat down at the desk. She typed a few words into Google. "435 dollars for the ounce."

Mike was the fastest. He had to do a lot of calculations on the fly during his job. "Wow... that's more than a quarter of a million dollars worth of gold in each box!"

Jia leaned back and put her arm around Mike's shoulders. She kissed him tenderly on the forehead. "My little genius." She smiled at Dean.

Dean got up and looked out the window. "So is there another way out of here? Or do we just send Karen out first to kick their ass?"

20

Photo #8

The man was lying on the bed, stretched
out. He was fully dressed, only his jacket
was missing. A knife was sticking in his
breast with only the handle visible.

He was framed by a large window behind the
bed with a busy river scene being played out
by many boats and ships of all sizes. The
white sails of the sampans and the puffs of
steam from the ships glowed in the sunlight.

21

THEY WALKED OUT through the back exit of the Scotland Residence, through an interior court yard and into the Highlands Hotel next door. The hotel was brand new like the residence building, aiming for immediate five-star status. A bewildering amount of staff was on hand everywhere, but nobody paid the four friends much attention as they walked through the lobby and out the front door where they flagged down a taxi.

Mike was looking out the back window while Jia was folding her long body into the backseat next to him. "I'm not seeing anybody observing us. Did anybody else see our friends in blue?"

"No, I think they just haven't figured this place out yet. But they are thorough, and I'm not sure how often we'll be able to pull this off." Dean was sitting next to the driver and now turned to him. "To the Suzhou Hotel, please?" He spoke slowly, since he had discovered two years ago that most taxi drivers in Shanghai did not speak much English.

The driver just nodded silently and hurtled the taxi down the driveway and out into the chaotic traffic, hitting the start button on the taxi meter nonchalantly. They were heading east towards the Bund, so Dean figured that the driver had understood.

WHILE THEY WERE driving downtown towards the oldest and densest populated part of Shanghai, Karen was again transfixed by the scenes on the street around them. She thought she could probably just sit there in a café with a view of the street and not move for days at a time, just letting life pass by.

They turned left into the new boulevard that now ran along the Bund and the view opened up into a gigantic panorama of old Shanghai on her left and the skyscraper-studded skyline on the other side of the river on her right. Her mouth formed a silent "O" and her eyes went big.

Jia had been watching her and now turned to Mike for a silent grin of pride for her hometown. Jia turned back. "All the buildings you see on the other side of the river? That area is called Pudong and it is all new development. When I was a little child, there was nothing but old warehouses over on the other side."

"Wow." Was all Karen could say.

The sun had come out and the glass and steel buildings on the other side of the Pujiang River reflected the light in a orgy of multi-hued flashes.

THEY MOVED NORTH along the Bund towards the old steel structure that bridges Soochow Creek at its mouth into the Pujiang, the main river that runs through Shanghai.

Dean pointed ahead at the bridge and turned to Karen. "Look. Reminds you of something?"

"Yes! You are right! That is the bridge in the pictures."

"The concrete bridge next to it is maybe only ten years old, but this bridge has been here for almost a century. And look over on the other side – that is the Compton House."

Karen had again the feeling that she had when they arrived in Shanghai – her granddad's stories were suddenly coming to life!

Anthony and Estelle must have been walking across this bridge a hundred times. Her granddad and grandma as young lovers, hand in hand. They had probably stopped there in the middle to look at the river traffic. They had kissed right there. Her head turned to look at the center of the bridge where, in her mind's eye, she saw her grandparents.

The taxi slowed down, turned right, and stopped in front of the entrance of the Suzhou Hotel. They got out of the stuffy taxi while Dean paid the driver, slowly counting out the unfamiliar bills.

THE FOUR OF them stood next to each other, looking up at the ancient facade of the building. Not much had changed in half a century. Her grandparents would have been right at home if they would see it now. It seemed that now also for the first time some money was being spent on the appearance of the building and several workers were busily painting window frames along one side.

Dean had pulled out the photos and pointed down the street that was running along Soochow Creek. "The trucks must have been stopped and plundered down that way, maybe three, four hundred feet down the road, close to the Shanghai Mansions." He was referring to the large brownstone tower that had been the Compton House's neighbor since before World War II.

Dean looked at the entrance of the hotel. The old signage was gone, but not much else had changed. The old lobby had been split into two several years ago once the economic boom had set in. The left side of the building's ground floor now hosted the Shanghai Stock Exchange trading floor, to the right was the entrance to the now smaller hotel lobby. Dean started to laugh. "You do realize that we are going to try and steal gold treasure out of the building of the Shanghai Stock Exchange."

Mike was laughing at that thought. "Karen, what room did your grandfather mention in his letter?"

"517. Should we just go in and ask if we can see the room?"

Jia started walking towards the building. "We can try."

THEY ENTERED THE lobby which also seemed to be frozen in time. The walls were covered in dark wood paneling and art deco style lamps were hanging from the ceiling. But instead of the distinguished guests of the past, a pair of young backpackers was sitting on a bench to one side of the check-in counter, intensively studying their guide book.

Jia walked up to counter and started a rapid exchange in Chinese with the staff. Mike gave a running translation of the conversation.

"Oh – that's good. Jia told them we are location scouts for a Hollywood movie. She has been asking if we can look at room 517... but the girl says that all the rooms on the fifth floor are rented out as offices... mostly for traders from the Stock Exchange, but also to other companies. And it seems that..."

Jia turned around "You will not believe who is renting 517!" Her eyes had turned big.

Karen looked at her unbelievingly. "No way! Yau?"

"Yes, the suites 515, 517 and 519 are rented by ShanghaiTrans. They've been using these rooms for years."

Dean looked aside at the travelers to make sure they were busy with their guide book and kept his voice low. "So... he must have known something. He probably found out in what room Peter Koshitzky had been murdered, or he heard some rumors from people who knew the gang that stole his stuff. He knew that something was up, but couldn't put it all together. He didn't have the pictures or Karen's letter."

Karen was disappointed. "But by now he must have searched the room pretty thoroughly. I mean, he had enough time to lift all the floorboards and look behind all the walls. What chance would we have anyway to find that stuff?"

Mike raised an eyebrow. "I don't think that three trucks worth of valuables would be in the room itself. I think I know how we can do our investigation and I think I have a pretty good idea where the boxes went."

He turned to the reception desk and asked something in fluent Chinese. He turned to his friends with a key in hand. "Just to get a feeling for this place, let's take a look at 417 first."

THE CORRIDORS OF the hotel didn't seem to have changed at all since the 1940s. Dark wood paneling, stained glass windows at strategic points, old art deco light fixtures that were in desperate need of repair. There were other signs of disrepair and rushed fixes that did not fit the interior, but large parts of the hotel seemed to have just emerged from a time warp. Dean wanted to urgently take pictures, just to preserve this glimpse into a different time.

Room 417 turned out to be an exact copy of the room in the photos. There was no oriental rug and no fireplace, but there was a bed near the window and two chairs and a small table against the wall.

Karen looked around with goosebumps on her arms. "This place is creepy. Wherever I look, I see things that my grandfather always talked about. And this room – it is so similar to the one in the pictures." She walked over the window. "Dean, can I have the pictures that show the view from 517?"

Dean came over and they both compared the view with the one in the photos. "This is great. So many of the old buildings are still there. And the two rivers don't seemed to have changed at all – they are still busy as hell."

Mike had joined them and opened the window. He leaned out, holding onto a metal railing that went along the outside of the windows and looked around, up and down. He came back in.

"This is the fourth window over from the corner near the bridge."

Dean looked at him. "So what's your plan? You want to climb up the wall to 517 tonight?"

Mike gave him his most harmless smile. "No. But I feel some emergency repairs coming up. Our cell phone transmitter on the roof of this building is clearly malfunctioning. I'll come over tomorrow afternoon and fix it."

22

"HMMM... THOSE APPETIZERS are tasty!" Karen was wolfing down the food, she was so hungry. They had not had any lunch and in their rush to see the Compton House with their own eyes they had completely forgotten about food.

They had crossed under the river with the Shanghai subway and Mike had brought them to the Pudong Garden Hotel, a 38 story hotel and apartment complex with a revolving restaurant at top. The hotel was close to the river and granted perfect views of Shanghai's old skyline along the Bund, the modern high rise buildings in the vast downtown area, and during one revolution also a breathtaking view of the postmodern metropolis that Pudong itself had become.

Every twenty minutes or so they had a view of the Compton House hotel across the river, easily recognizable because of the mouth of Soochow Creek just next to it, with the signature span of the steel bridge pointing directly at the hotel. Dean could not stop staring at the hotel. A kiss on his cheek from Karen brought him back to the real world. "Wake up." She said softly.

He kissed her back, tasting the Teriyaki flavor of the appetizers on her lips.

"Hmmm... tastes good!" He leaned forward. Karen put her index finger on his lips. She smiled with a promise for later in her eyes.

Mike cleared his throat. "So, uh... did we tell you we got engaged?"

Karen turned to them "Really? That is so great! When are you planning to marry?"

"Oh, in September. The weather then is so much nicer if we are lucky and hit a break between two Typhoons."

Karen looked at them. "How did you meet? I take it in Shanghai?"

Jia smiled at the memories. "I had just started my MBA studies and I was working most nights as a bartender in the bar of the Highlands Hotel. When Mike moved into the residence apartment next door he often came by for a drink. I guess he was afraid to go somewhere else at night." She laughed and Mike gave her a fake slap on the back of her head. "And I think he was a bit shy with girls, too." Another fake slap. But he also had to smile at these memories. "But I kind of liked him... so I asked him out."

Karen whooped loudly and people at the other tables were looking at the misbehaving foreigners. "Way to go, girl!" Karen and Jia high-fived each other across the table.

"SO WHAT DID your parents say?"

Jia's face became a little darker. "First they seemed not to mind at all. My mom liked the idea that he was American." She took a sip from her Mai Tai and continued. "But then they figured out that he was Japanese American. They were screaming at me, and begging me to stop seeing him, my mom was crying. It was horrible." During her description Mike had been gently rubbing her shoulder. "It took almost a year before they even wanted to talk about him again. By then Mike's Chinese had become excellent and we worked hard to get my parents to meet him.

Finally they invited Mike for dinner – in their house!" She turned to look at Mike. "And once they saw him and talked to him, they completely turned around. It was the most amazing thing!"

"Yeah, especially your mom seems to like me a lot." Mike said.

"You bet. When I visit, that's the first thing she asks – 'How is Mike? Is he OK? Does he eat enough?'" Jia laughed.

"So how much longer do you have to study for your MBA?" Dean asked.

Meanwhile the food had arrived and they all started eating like they were starving.

"Another year. I hope I'll be able to find a job with one of the international companies here in town. But it's a tough job market. Every Chinese wants to work in Shanghai."

Karen looked up from the food. "How about coming to the States?"

"Not so easy. Even once we are married, it will take a while to get a Green Card. Too many Chinese are applying, so there is a long waiting list."

FOR A WHILE they were all eating in silence. They had ordered Asian fusion food, family style, and there were half a dozen different dishes to discover.

Dean couldn't wait any longer. "So Mike, how do you want to pull this off tomorrow?"

"I have to work tomorrow morning, and while I'm out on the job, I can always call into our headquarters and ask them if anybody else had been getting bad signal strengths from the transmitter on the Suzhou Hotel. And then I tell them that I'll be in the neighborhood later, and they will call the hotel and tell them that somebody is going to be over to do some maintenance work on the antennas on their roof. That's pretty standard and they won't be worried about it."

"And how do we get into the room?"

"We count the windows to make sure that we get the right room and then we climb down through the chimney. You've seen the picture of that fireplace in room 517. That chimney has got to be a huge pipe straight up to the roof. I'll bring the climbing gear — we use that regularly to access some of the more challenging roof locations."

Jia looked up expectantly. "We?"

"No, not 'We'. Just Dean and me. It's not that I don't trust you to be able to do this, but if there's suddenly four strangers with climbing gear heading for the roof, the hotel staff may get a bit suspicious."

"Ohhh! You just want to have all the fun for yourself." Jia pouted.

AFTER DINNER THEY took a taxi back to the Scotland Residence, rolling through downtown Shanghai with its neon-lit streets. It was obvious to Karen that this was a boomtown, showing off its newfound wealth and sophistication. The streets were crowded with people enjoying the mild evening temperatures for a little stroll, eating ice cream, some window shopping.

The taxi stopped in front of the Residence. Getting out of the car, all four of them were scanning the street nervously. Dean was the first to speak. "All clear. It seems our friends got bored — or hungry."

Karen was hopeful. "Maybe they gave up. They saw us enter the building, but maybe they figured they'd lost us on the way out. They couldn't know we would actually come back and stay here for the night."

"Yeah. Let's hope you are right."

23

DEAN WAS TRYING to squeeze himself into a red work overall between a tiny workbench and a storage container for electrical parts in the back of a bouncing Toyota minivan. The overall, the van, and all the tools and boxes were dark red and had a huge white DynaRola "D" on them. Mike was already wearing the same company overall and he was driving the van with wild abandon through Shanghai's busy afternoon traffic.

"You know that you will never again be able to drive a car in the States? They'd lock you up for attempted manslaughter on your first day back."

Mike laughed and shouted back to Mike across the noise of the engine. "I know. The way they drive cars in this country is something else. I almost peed my pants the first day I had to drive by myself in this place. The trick is mostly to relax and to ignore everything else on the street, including the traffic lights." Just to make his point, he drove across a red light, completely ignoring the oncoming city bus, the school kids on bikes between him and the bus, the old woman with the impossibly big basket of vegetables on her back, the red minitaxi speeding past and a dozen other distractions, and drove the van straight across the busiest intersection Dean had ever seen without even touching the brake.

Dean had to will himself to let go of the edge of the workbench. "Wow. Don't do that again."

"What?"

"I said... oh, never mind!" He crawled forward between the seats and dropped into the passenger seat, making sure he locked the seatbelt correctly.

DEAN HAD BEEN waiting in front of the Highlands Hotel and Mike had picked him up at around three o'clock. After making sure that they were not being followed, they were now on their way to the Suzhou Hotel.

They had just crossed Soochow Creek and they were approaching the old Compton House along the same little road that followed the river that the trucks with Yau's gold had taken so many years ago.

They parked around the corner and walked in, receiving the key for the roof access from the front desk. Both of them were carrying assorted tool bags and each had a backpack with climbing equipment, digital cameras, flash lights and other gear they thought could come in handy.

After five floors up on the main stairwell they switched to a utility staircase in the back of the building which continued further up for two more floors, until they finally reached the access door to the roof.

DEAN WAS BREATHING hard. "This stuff is heavy. I mean, I'm carrying around some 15 pounds of camera equipment almost everywhere I go, but this is at least double that."

"Yeah. It keeps me in shape. And this is actually not so bad. There are a few places in town where we have to lug everything up 10 floors of narrow stairs." Mike had already tried the first two keys on the ring he got from the girl at the desk, but then the third one turned and the narrow door opened to a small terrace. They dragged their gear outside and Mike closed and locked the door behind them.

Dean looked around. The roof was a confusing maze of gables and spires with narrow iron-grating walkways between them. Chimneys of all sizes peppered the roof landscape. On one side a large glass roof covered an inner courtyard and Dean made a mental note to not get too close to that area. Mike started unpacking several devices and some of his tools.

"I'll actually do some maintenance on the transmitter over there." He pointed at a 20-foot mast that crowned a nearby spire. It had a large DynaRola sign attached to it and a smaller one that announced 'Danger – Do Not Touch – High Voltage'.

"I won't need your help, I guess, so relax and enjoy your stay in – or as it happens on top of - the Suzhou Hotel."

Dean had brought his digital camera and had already started to take advantage of this unique opportunity to shoot Shanghai from an unusual angle. "Yep. Don't worry about me. There is a lot to see from up here."

24

AFTER A RESTFUL night and a good breakfast Karen felt rejuvenated. Not being involved in today's excursion to the roof of the Suzhou hotel didn't bother her too much. It had been a very hectic week and she still had not fully adjusted to this new existence as an adventuress and treasure hunter in a romantic relationship while running from the Hong Kong mafia.

She had finally called her parents and told them that she had changed her plans and would be staying away a little while longer. She was careful not to destroy the impression that she may still be in San Francisco. She just couldn't find the words to explain intelligently what had happened to her life lately.

Karen had also remotely changed the message on her answering machine so that her clients knew she would be out of town a little while longer. It was just after tax season, so she didn't expect any of her regular clients to call her until sometime in autumn anyway.

JIA WALKED AROUND the apartment restlessly. "You want to come along to visit my parents' place?" She turned back from the window. "Nobody is watching the building. I guess you were right last night. They must be looking elsewhere for you."

Karen laughed nervously. "I'm not sure if I should feel good about a bunch of gangsters running around town looking for me. But I guess it is better than actually having them wait in front of the house." She had been surfing the Web, but now she got up from the desk and stretched. A mild crackling pop emitted from her back. "Ouch! I'm getting old. OK, let's go. I'm in Shanghai – I want to see something of this town, gangsters or not!"

They left the building through the hotel and walked along a busy shopping street for a few blocks before turning into a small side street. Shanghai had historically been a divided city with different areas being influenced by the various colonial powers who had settled there. Many of these differences were still visible and Karen enjoyed discovering the flavor of each neighborhood.

These side streets where Jia had grown up had not yet been touched by the rapid urban renewal that was so evident along the major roads. The small, dark alleys reminded Karen a lot of some of neighborhoods she had seen in Paris and other French cities.

CURRENTLY THEY WERE wading through a tide of school children running the other way. "That is where I went to school, too!" Jia shouted over the noise of the excited 6-year olds. Some of the children tried to stop to look at Karen, but the stream of children pushed them forward and past the exotic foreigner wandering through their world.

Karen tried to imagine Jia as one of the children, but couldn't – Jia was such a vividly beautiful woman, it was hard to think of her in any other way. "Have you ever thought of modeling? You certainly have the body for it."

"Well, when I was still working as a bartender, I had been approached quite often, but it was hard to figure out if these offers were serious. Men will say the stupidest things to a female bartender!" She looked back at Karen. "I don't know. I never thought of myself as special... I think I would be uncomfortable to see myself in a lingerie advertisement."

Karen had to laugh at that thought. She noticed that away from the main streets, the local population was not expecting to see foreigners. Some people seemed surprised and openly stared at her.

Jia saw her worried look and laughed. "Don't worry about people staring. They are probably mostly worried about you being lost back here."

THE BUILDINGS IN these side streets were all from the colonial times and in many cases had only received the most basic maintenance over the past decades. Jia turned to the right through a small, narrow passage and led Karen through a dark and moldy tunnel into a sunny backyard with several tall trees, their trunks surrounded by potted flowers and a few small vegetable plots. The trees created leafy, ever-changing shadows across the yard. A smaller two-story house stood in the backyard hunched up against another building.

"That's my family's place." Jia's eyes glittered with pride.

"Four generations live under this roof. My grandma, my parents, and my little sister with her husband and their baby-boy."

"Oh – so you are auntie Jia?" Karen laughed. "Sorry, but none of my aunts ever looked so hip!"

Jia smiled. "Very funny!" She started waving. "There's my mother." She shouted something in Chinese.

25

DEAN LOOKED DOWN into the gaping mouth of the chimney. "You sure this is the right one?"

They stood in the twilight behind a steep gable that protected them from view from the streets, with a row of large chimneys along the steep side of the roof.

"We've counted the windows twice and there's only so many possible chimneys. This must be it." Mike leaned against the brick chimney, which had the outer dimensions of a phone booth. "These rooms on the top floor facing the water were the premier suites of the hotel. They each had a separate fire place with a chimney leading straight up through the attic and the roof. Now let's see... winner goes down first." He held out a fist.

It took Dean a moment to realize what Mike wanted. He also held out a fist. They shook their fists up and down, looking each other in the eyes. Their eyes dropped.

"Scissors."

"Paper. Damn, OK, you go first, I'll spot you." Mike picked up the climbing rope and gave one end to Dean who started securing it to his climbing belt.

Dean had done a lot of rock climbing in the Sierra Nevada when he was in college and also once a few years back for a week-long photo assignment in a cave in the Swiss Alps. So he was confident about his climbing, but he was a bit worried about the stability of the chimney. At least he had a DynaRola-branded construction helmet that they had rigged up with a flashlight attached to it with silvery duct tape.

They checked each other's rope work and Mike switched on Dean's helmet light. "Ready?"

"Ready." They had already unscrewed the little metal roof that protected the chimney from rain. Dean took the roof off and carefully put it down in the sharp angle between chimney and roof tiles. He pulled himself up to the edge of the chimney, his feet banging once against the metal roof, and then he sat on the edge with his feet dangling into the dark void.

The inside dimensions were just about perfect for a caving session. It was a rectangular shaft of two by four feet. The walls were rough brick with easy grooves between the individual bricks. Everything was covered with black soot, but it had been stuck to the walls for so long, it had turned into a hard crust.

Dean tapped the walkie-talkie that was hanging on his shoulder. Both his and Mike's beeped at the same time. "OK, let's do this." He slowly moved the center point of his body over the shaft, put his feet into the brick grooves and moved down, experimentally putting some of his weight on the rope. It was easier than he had thought. He was wearing thin leather gloves that gave his hands enough protection from the sharp edges, and he got a good grip on the walls.

HE BRACED HIS body across the long side of the chimney and descended in a slow backward walk. He tried to not kick too much dirt down into the fireplace. It was completely dark down there. He had already been wondering about that. He took a second flashlight from a small backpack that he carried on his breast and pointed it straight down.

He put the flash light back and pushed the walkie talkie to his mouth. "Mike?" He looked up. The sky was a small, very dark purple rectangle above him. The climbing rope was taut and disappeared over the edge.

"Yeah. Everything cool down there?"

"Yeah, it's going pretty well actually. Listen, the fireplace is not being used anymore. Something is blocking it off, could be either a wall, or some boards or furnishing, something. I can't see that yet. It's at least another twenty feet to the fireplace."

"Interesting. Well, if my theory is correct, then we don't even have to go into the room. Have you seen anything else?"

"Just dirty bricks. Talk to you in a minute." Dean clicked off and started moving down again slowly. He realized that the excitement of the climb had made him forget about examining the walls, as Mike had asked him to. He looked up along the walls on all sides, but it seems he hadn't missed anything yet.

HE HAD CLIMBED down another six feet when his back suddenly did not touch anything anymore. He let out a gasp.

His back hit against wood and his head connected with a sharp brick edge, just under the helmet. He slid another foot, and his head was now banging against the wooden wall behind him, before he was able to brace himself with his hands. Mike had noticed the movement and the rope had become taut at the same time.

Dean was breathing hard. Small, sooty crumbs of all sorts had fallen in his face and eyes. He had to convince himself that he was in no danger. He willed his breathing to slow down. He explored under himself with one foot, letting Mike hold his weight for a moment. There was a sill under him. He turned and braced himself facing the other way, with his feet now resting on the sill.

"Mike!"

"What happened down there? For a moment I thought..."

"I'm OK. You were right. There is a fucking door in the chimney shaft!"

Silence from the roof.

"Wow. Locked?"

"No idea yet. It's in a niche on one of the narrow sides of the shaft..." Dean had pulled his digital camera out of the backpack and was taking pictures.

"Are you taking pictures?"

Dean had heard Mike's laughter over the walkie talkie. "Yes, why?"

"Oh nothing – I saw the flash going off in the chimney. Can't wait to see your snapshots."

"And the door is locked, there is a big lock that hooks through two metal loops on the door and wall. The door is about two by five feet and opens to the room behind it. The only way through is to get rid of the lock. Which, by the way, looks like it is at least fifty years old."

Dean examined the lock for a little while. It was big and rusty and parallel lines on the front plate created an art deco pattern. It looked like it was straight from the nineteen thirties.

"Listen, I'm in a very comfortable position here. My feet are pushing against the door sill. If you can secure the rope somewhere up there, you could pass me a small metal saw down on a second line and I'll get this lock out of the way in no time."

"OK. Hang on." The rope was dangling left and right in front of Dean's nose, went slightly lose and stayed that way. He looked down and saw now that there seemed to be furniture blocking the fireplace. It looked like the backside of a large metal filing cabinet.

"You still there?"

"Yep. I'm enjoying the view."

"Look up. The saw is coming your way."

Dean looked up and there was a small metal saw coming down on a much thinner line. It occurred to him that thanks to Mike's job they had been perfectly equipped for this operation.

"Got it!" He untied the saw and the empty line quickly snaked up and away.

"You better take up the slack on my line again. I'll need both my hands for this one."

"No problem." His rope was taut again.

He started sawing through the lock. It had been a good lock for its time, but after rusting for more than five decades it was no match for the little saw with its high-tech blade. There was surprisingly little noise, but Dean doubted that anybody would have heard him in here anyway, even if he would have used a sledgehammer.

He was sawing furiously for another couple of minutes and suddenly he was through. He put the saw into his backpack and twisted the lock to pull it out of the metal bands. He was breathing hard again. "Come on Dean, there is nothing behind this door anyway. Calm down." He whispered under his breath.

DEAN TOOK THE lock and deposited it in the backpack as a souvenir. It was after all his first break-in. He braced himself against the other side of the chimney and pushed with one hand against the door. It didn't move at all. He leaned back against the wall and pushed with one foot. There was a little give, but not much.

"Come on!" he pushed with all his power and suddenly the door snapped open. The air changed. It was like cold and hot air was coming through the door at the same time. Dean shivered. A cloud of dust enveloped him, reducing visibility to less than a foot. He started coughing.

"Dean, are you OK? What's going on down there?"

Dean was breathing into his overall. More coughing. "Hold on Mike, there's just a lot of dust. I kicked the door open! But I can't see a thing right now..."

Slowly the dust thinned, with the heavier particles drifting down and the light ones being drawn up into the chimney.

"So... Can you see *something?*" Mike sounded very unhappy about not being able to take a look himself.

Dean grabbed the door frame on both sides and pulled himself through.

"Mike. I'm in."

26

KAREN HAD THOROUGHLY enjoyed the afternoon with Jia's family. Jia's mother was a tiny woman, just under five feet with a round, kind face with a landscape of wrinkles around the eyes. But she had the same fiery spirit as Jia and there was no doubt that they were mother and daughter.

They had fed her local delicacies and Jia's mother and grandmother had started to dig through boxes full of childhood photos of Jia, very much to Jia's chagrin.

It had started to turn dark outside, and both Karen's and Jia's thoughts turned to what Mike and Dean were doing.

"Please tell your mother that I'm very thankful for the beautiful afternoon and the great food. Uhm... how do you say thank you again? *Xie-xie!*"

Jia translated everything. Her mother got up from the table and took Karen's hand and arm in both her hands. She just smiled at Karen and said something. Jia laughed. "She said, she hopes next time we bring our boyfriends along."

Karen laughed at that, hugged both Jia's mother and grandmother, and then she followed Jia out of the house, across the yard and out into the dark street.

CHINESE BACKALLEYS WERE still a new experience for Karen. Small, dim light bulbs lit the entrances to the the buildings and there were only a few street lights fighting against the encroaching darkness at some of the street corners. Bikes had no lights on them and even most motor scooters and cars used their headlights only when they came up to an intersection.

A man on a bike flew past like a bat. "Is it always that dark in the cities?"

"Yeah, I guess you could say it is traditional. The government has been trying to educate at least the car drivers to keep their lights on, but many people think they save energy by not using their lights all the time."

Just to make her point, a small truck drove up to them, flashed its lights briefly to warn them and then zoomed past, all dark again.

"Whoa. That was close. I think I'll skip biking at night."

"It's a lot brighter out on the main streets. Here in Shanghai only the back streets are so dark."

She was right. In fact, the difference was remarkable. All the shops had bright lights and huge neon signs, with music blasting from quite a few of the shop fronts.

They strolled down the street, looking at some of the displays.

Karen sighed. "I'm not really in the mood for window shopping. I'm thinking of Dean and Mike all the time."

"Yes. Me too. Let's go back to the apartment."

They turned down the street that ran past the front of the Scotland Residence. This area had become more quiet after dark and there were only a few bikers and the odd taxi on the road.

THERE WAS A small street-side restaurant two buildings away from the residence, and the owner and his only waitress came out to greet them. Jia waved and shouted something about

Karen, pointing at her. Karen took that as cue for a friendly smile and wave. The owner laughed and waved back. Some of his patrons looked at them over their shoulders.

"That's Cheng. He's a really nice guy and his food is great. We come here sometimes for a quick snack. He loves to chat with Mike."

"Nice guy..."

A BLACK LIMOUSINE drove past, slowed, swerved right and cut off their way to the apartment building. Two men jumped out, their sunglasses dark in the night. Jia screamed and Karen took a step back away from the man that was coming after her.

"Help!" As her kick-boxing teacher had told her once, when being attacked, screaming never hurts. The man had come in range and she had taken up a fighting stance. She lashed out with her right foot twice. Face. Groin. She retreated a few steps, while the man let out all his air in one loud groan, falling forward, his sunglasses describing a lazy arc through the air, crashing into the roof of the limousine.

The other man had his arms wrapped around Jia and was trying to drag her into the car, but she was considerably taller than him and was furiously kicking at his knees and feet, making loud popping noises where her shoes connected with his bones. Jia was screaming Chinese invective at the attackers.

Karen lunged forward, jumping over her attacker who was trying to get up while holding his groin. She kicked the man who was wrestling with Jia in the right kidney. She heard shouts behind her and turned around to fend off the first man again, when she saw Cheng, the chef of the restaurant, running down the street with an enormous meat cleaver in his hands. Several of his male guests were running after him, albeit a bit more cautious than him.

Her first attacker had come up fast when he saw the chef with the cleaver running at him full speed. He jumped backward towards the car, a maneuver Karen had not anticipated, and his elbow hit her chin, sending her backwards into Jia and the other man. There were urgent shouts from the driver.

Karen had gone down, turned on her back and kicked upwards at the man still holding Jia. She hit his arm hard and something cracked loudly – he let go and screamed. Jia had been off her feet and fell on top of Karen, knocking the wind out of her.

Cheng had come swinging the cleaver, missing the second attacker by an inch. The man had just gotten his arm broken and had now almost been beheaded. That seemed to be enough for him and he jumped into the limousine after his colleague, pulling the door shut with his good arm. His continuing scream of pain was cut off by the door.

The car took off with tires squealing in protest. It hurtled down the street and turned left, out of sight, at the next corner.

CHEF CHENG HAD dropped the cleaver and was pulling Jia up from Karen. The other men had arrived and gave Karen a hand. Finally they stood in a circle of chattering men, with Karen feeling disoriented and scared and not understanding a single word. She wanted to lie down. What was the word for Thank You again?

Jia had started to thank everybody. She was leaning against Karen, and both of them started moving towards the apartment with the men surrounding them like bodyguards.

Karen and Jia both hugged Cheng and shook the other three men's hands and walked into the Scotland Residence. Nobody had proposed to call the police and Karen was glad about it. The last thing she wanted to do right now was explaining to the cops why she was here and what they were up to.

THERE WAS A mirror between the doors of the two elevators and Karen and Jia looked at each other while they waited for one of the elevators to slowly ping-ping its way down to the ground floor. They both were dirty and had gotten a scratch here and there, but they had survived in a lot better shape than the two men. They started laughing hysterically.

In the elevator, Jia hugged Karen. "You were amazing out there! You saved me from that guy! Thank You, Thank You, Thank You!"

"Oh, you did pretty well, too. That guy is not going to walk much tomorrow."

The elevator opened on the sixth floor, spilling their relieved laughter out into the corridor. They got out and turned to their apartment door.

They could hear a phone ringing through the door. Jia's hands were shaking badly and she needed several tries to jam the key into the lock and turn it. She sprinted to the desk and grabbed the phone.

"Wei!"

Karen was closing the door carefully, locking it and turned around.

"It's Mike! Dean has found something!" Jia put the phone back up. "Wait, wait, wait! You are talking so fast... What? There's a door in the chimney? And a room? The computer... yeah, it's sleeping. I'll wake it up." She touched the mouse and the flat screen came to live with a desktop background image of Shanghai's skyline at night that Mike had taken while working on a transmitter on top of one of Asia's tallest buildings. Jia opened a web browser and started typing. "One-Ninetyseven...one-twentynine... fifteen. OK."

She turned to Karen behind her. "Dean is in a secret room in the Suzhou Hotel and he is sending live images from a PDA to

Mike's laptop on the roof! We'll be able to watch it from here!" Her eyes were glittering with excitement.

"What? Right now?" Karen felt like an idiot. She was using computers every day at work, but this was way beyond anything she had seen before. And Dean was in a *secret room*? What did that mean?

"Can you put Mike on speaker phone?"

"Oh – good idea." Jia hit a button on the phone and hung up. "Mike? We are on speaker phone."

Mike's disembodied voice filled the room. "Hi Karen. Welcome to our little chatline." he sounded exuberant, almost like he had been drinking.

A picture had just appeared on the screen. Jia enlarged it to fullscreen. It was a picture of a dark room with the beams from two flashlights stabbing through the dusty air. There were boxes and indistinguishable shapes everywhere. Now the picture changed. More boxes. And again. They seemed to get a new picture every two seconds or so.

A beep through the phone and they heard Dean's distorted voice. "There is so much stuff down here. It will take a long time to even figure out what this all is!"

Mike's voice again. "Roger that. And we have the girls on the phone and Internet now, so they'll be able to hear and see you. But there is no backchannel, so I'll do the talking for them."

"Really? Hi there! This is live from the treasure chamber!"

It was ridiculous, but Karen's eyes filled with tears. For the first time she felt that this was *her* Dean!

27

DEAN WAS HAPPY that Karen could see this. He had barely made it through the door when his shin hit the sharp edge of a stack of boxes. Dust was everywhere. Every time he moved, clouds of nasty, fine dust took his breath away. He had spent a few minutes to set up the PDA with the tiny camera so that it was sitting on that first stack of boxes, facing along the length of the room. The wireless connection with Mike's laptop was no problem, since only a thin roof separated the two.

"Mike, the room has no doors. I mean, no other doors."

"How is that possible? What kind of architect builds a room with no doors?"

"I guess that this attic was not supposed to be used for anything. Or maybe that wall that you can see there towards the far end, maybe that has been added later to create this room."

"Possible. The picture from you PDA is not very clear. There's too much dust. Can you describe a bit more what is down there?"

"Sure." Dean turned slowly on his heels, for the first time trying to take it all in. He was not even aware that he had entered the frame of the PDA's camera.

Karen five miles away was ecstatic. "Oh! It's Dean." She moved forward to get a closer look, bumping shoulders with Jia. Both were completely lost in the pixelated picture before them.

DEAN TRIED TO sum up everything he saw. "The room is about fifteen feet wide and forty feet long and has a sloping roof all the way down to the floor boards. This is pretty much a part of the fake gables of the hotel that you can see from the bridge. The wall at the far end is raw brick. There is only the one door that I've used to enter. The floor is wood, but solid and it doesn't creak when I move. There is a lot of dust. And I mean *a lot!* About half an inch of it on every flat surface."

"There are many boxes here. Some are small and massive like the ones close to the door that the PDA is now sitting on. They seem to be very heavy. Then there are others, in different shapes. Some are kind of long with a square cross section. That could be rolled up documents or artwork. There is actually quite a lot of these longer ones... maybe a hundred or so."

"None of the items that I can see is longer than 5 feet and so all of them could have come here from room 517 and up through the chimney."

He had now almost finished one 360 degree turn and was looking at the wall behind the chimney where he had entered.

"Oh."

He walked over and kneeled down. "And I'm not alone. Well, relatively speaking."

"What?"

"No, don't worry. But there is a skeleton down here."

Dean was not too uncomfortable with a skeleton in the room. He had once spent a night taking pictures in a morgue for a magazine and that had been much more of a horror trip. This one at least had already been dead for half a century.

Mike's voice came back. "Nonono... he's ok. Hey, Dean. Do you want to say something? I have two very worried women screaming in my ear."

"I'm ok, really! This guy is not going to do much anytime soon." He was still on one knee in front of the dead man. The flashlight on his helmet was always aiming slightly off from where he wanted to see, so he had to move his head around a lot. He slowly took in everything about the man.

THE SKELETON WAS sitting against the wall, legs stretched out. He was wearing dark pants and a dark vest with a white shirt, no jacket. Black leather shoes were sideways on the ground where his feet had been. A dark brown stain was visible all the way down the front of the shirt. There was a rope knotted around the breast of the man, now a loose loop hanging down with the rest of the rope neatly tucked behind the body.

"I think I found Peter."

"Peter? Who are you talking about?"

"Remember the letter Karen's grandfather wrote? The dead guy on the photo, his name was Peter so-and-so. This is him!" Dean got up again and looked at the position of the body. "It makes sense. If the police or the communist militia would have found the dead man in the room, they would have done a thorough job checking out room 517 and may have discovered this attic.

I guess Karen's grandfather was incredibly lucky – after he had taken the pictures and left, the people who had stolen Yau's money came back and removed the body. But it was during the day, they were in a hurry. You can't just drag the body of a stabbed man through a hotel. So they did the next best thing and pulled him up into the chimney and stashed him in here with the loot."

Dean had taken out his camera and took several pictures of the body of Peter Koshitzky, and enough shots to later assemble a full panorama of the room from this standpoint.

"Dean, we'll need some sort of clue what all this stuff is. Can you check some of the boxes?"

"Exactly my thoughts." He went to a stack of boxes near the one with the PDA on top, so they could all see what he was doing. He smiled at the camera.

FIVE MILES AWAY the smile made Karen blush. This was his smile for her. He looked pretty dashing with the soot-streaked overall and the helmet with the flashlight taped to it. Her boyfriend, the treasure hunter.

Dean tried to lift the top box, but it was incredibly heavy for its size, maybe 30 or 40 pounds. It was made from good wood, nothing like a modern shipping crate. The lid of the box had been secured with a metal band around the box with a small padlock on top. He pulled the saw out of the backpack. "Time for a little crafts presentation."

Mike was sitting on the roof, leaning against the chimney with the laptop on his knees. He was drinking from a water bottle while watching the small picture on the screen refresh every couple of seconds with a shot of Dean sawing through the padlock. The picture was yellowish dark, with strange, dusty patterns like ghosts hanging in the air behind Dean. Small LEDs at the bottom of the screen were blinking green and blue with every connection made by Dean's tiny PDA and Jia's Mac back home...

Back in the apartment, Karen and Jia sat at the desk in the dark. The grainy picture of Dean was filling the large flat screen, it's light a yellow glow in the faces of the two women. They were transfixed by the dance of light, shadow and dust behind Dean, sent to them one picture at a time...

JIA WAS WHISPERING. "...it looks like... ghosts." She grabbed Karen's arm. She was shuddering hard. "Do you see that!" Her voice was hoarse, she was breathing fast. Karen felt like cold water was trickling down her back. Her mouth opened and closed, opened and closed.

Mike's hand with the water bottle slowly sank to his side. He jerked when water dripped on his hand. The hairs on his neck were rising. He saw shapes in the dusty air. It felt like he had left his body and was seeing himself watch the video from above. He couldn't speak. He couldn't speak... his hand moved to the walkie-talkie in slow motion...

Dean was breathing hard, moving the saw back and forward in a smooth, rapid motion. Sweat was dripping of his nose.

He'd always been good with tools, even as a child. He wondered why he suddenly had this strange flashback to his childhood, working with the crafts set, one of the best Christmas presents ever. His dad had been so proud...

"Dean!"

HIS MIND SNAPPED back to the present. He gasped. The lock broke and his right hand with the saw jerked sideways. He could see what was happening, but it was too fast. His hand scraped along the sharp metal edge of the lock.

"Damn! Oh... damn!" Dean dropped the saw and instinctively pressed the cut into his mouth. He opened his fist and looked at the cut. Not too deep and it wasn't bleeding a lot, but it really hurt.

He hit the walkie-talkie. "What?" He had to wipe the sweat out of his eyes. He hadn't realized how hot it had become in the attic. He looked around and froze.

Shadows were slowly falling out of the dust. For a moment it had looked like people had been standing there.

"Mike." He realized he was whispering. He cleared his throat. "Mike!"

"Yes. You saw it too." It was not a question.

"I... I'm not sure what I saw. There is a lot of dust in the air." He looked down at his hand. The bleeding had already slowed down.

He turned back to the boxes and checked the flashlight. It was one of the new LED flashlights that last for dozens of hours and it was still as powerful as when he had switched it on.

Karen and Jia were holding each others hands. "Now they are gone." Jia was still whispering. She turned to Karen. "I'm not crazy, am I?"

"No... I saw it too. That was not just dust... there was *something*."

Mike's voice came over the phone. "Yeah, I saw it too." Both women shrank away in surprise. They had forgotten that Mike was still on the phone and could hear them.

Dean was back on the screen, checking the flashlight next to the PDA. His hands filled the screen. One of them was bloody. Karen felt lightheaded. What had they done? This was so much bigger than just a treasure hunt.

DEAN HAD TURNED his attention back to the box. He twisted the second lock he had broken during that night off the hinged metal belt. The belt opened lightly without any noise. He lifted the wooden lid and slowly set it down on the ground.

This was the moment when he was supposed to whistle appreciatively, or maybe to laugh maniacally. He had seen the movies. But all he wanted to do is turn to his left and look into the long shadows of the room, to see if the images in the dust would come back, to hunt him down and to... no. This was no movie. He looked anyway, but there was nothing, just dust motes dancing in the light.

He looked back down and lifted a gold bar out of the box. It was so much more heavy than anything of that size should be. He held it up in front of the PDA, turning it slowly. The bare yellow metal caught the intense beam of the light and flashes of gold were flicking trough the room. The metal felt soft and warm on his skin.

Mike's face and eyes reflected the yellow shine of the gold bar on the screen of his laptop. He hit the button. "Wow."

Dean shifted the weight to one hand and toggled the walkie-talkie. "Yes. This is what Yau wants."

IT WAS AFTER midnight when Dean pulled himself out of the narrow door and into the chimney. He was back on the climbing rope, but it was not taut yet. Mike was still pulling the other rope back up, with one of the document boxes attached. It was the third one.

Dean had randomly selected three of the long boxes and also two smaller, lighter square ones. Mike had pulled them out of the chimney without any problems. Dean had also put five of the gold bars into his backpack, as he didn't think that the backpack would be able to carry more of them, and pulling the heavy boxes filled with gold bars out of the room would need some planning and maybe also more equipment.

He pulled the door shut and finally started his ascent through the chimney. It was easy climbing, and only the ten pounds of gold hitting his spine every now and then made it problematic.

He reached the top and pulled himself over the edge. Mike held him by the shoulders while he slowly turned and lowered himself to the roof of the hotel. All around the glow of the skyscrapers brightened the night sky. Dean could hear cars down on the streets, a woman laughing. He was back in the world of the living. He and Mike shook hands.

They used several large DynaRola equipment bags that had been stored in a little locker next to the cell phone tower and wrapped the strong Tyvek material around the boxes, making two longish bundles that they then decorated with lengths of wires hanging out of the ends. They packed up all their equipment, leaving the climbing gear in the locker and entered the hotel through the roof door.

"I THINK I'LL keep this one." Mike pulled the key for the roof door off the keyring and dropped it into his wallet.

They descended the stairs with their heavy load of equipment and nonchalantly walked past the reception, just stopping long enough to drop off the keyring for the roof access. Mike was joking with the staff and earned some good-natured laughter.

They left the hotel. "They were not suspicious?"

"No – people everywhere in China are working long hours. Especially in construction and related fields like engineering, the work never ends in a country with 1.3 billion people and a booming economy."

"Speaking of China – we'll have to sit down and figure out what we are going to do here. We are sitting on a pile of gold and possibly ancient Chinese artworks and if the government ever finds out about us not telling them, we are going to be in deep, deep trouble."

"Yeah, I know." Mike was opening the rear door of the DynaRola van. He dropped the first Tyvek bundle into the van. "We shouldn't be doing..." The second bundle followed. "...what we are doing." They both threw their tool belts and backpacks next to the bundles and Mike slapped the door shut.

Mike looked at Dean with a crooked grin and shrugged. They both started laughing.

WHEN THEIR RED-AND-WHITE van disappeared around the corner, the shape of a man came out of the shadows. The man was tall and slender with a long, ascetic face under the hood of a flowing, orange robe.

They slowly drove past the apartment, but could not see anybody at all out on the street. Mike went down the ramp and parked the car in the garage of the complex next to his little red car. Behind them the huge automatic door rattled down and closed with a final metallic bang.

28

"MIKE!"

"Dean!"

The two woman were hugging their boyfriends. Boxes and backpacks clattered to the floor as the men found something better to do with their hands.

Dean resurfaced from an especially passionate kiss. "It's nice to see you again"

"Mhh-hmmm..." Karen looked at him. He was utterly dirty, with dust, metal particles and dried blood smeared across his forehead.

Dean realized what she was looking at. "Oh – I think I'll take a shower first. It was a little bit dusty down there."

Mike had been talking to Jia behind them and he now saw her left arm. "Hey honey! Where did you get that scratch from?"

"Oh yes! There is something we've got to tell you." Jia started.

"Yeah, we had our own adventure back at the ranch, you know?"

BOTH STARTED TALKING at the same time, pulling the two men in to the living room. "There were these two guys..." "The limousine just stopped..." "Karen kicked the guy..." "...and this guy from the restaurant comes running!" "I couldn't get away!" "...I was on the ground..." "Cheng almost killed the man!" "...the men were really helpful but I couldn't talk to them..."

Dean and Mike stared at them openmouthed, their own evening almost forgotten. They were terrified about the thought of almost losing their girlfriends in an abduction. When Karen and Jia finally stopped talking, it was quiet for a while.

They all looked at each other. Dean broke the silence first. "If we want to pull this off – and I'm not sure yet what exactly we are doing – we'll have to stay somewhere else."

"I have an idea." Mike smiled at them. Dean was reading his face. "Oh... Oh no. That is not what you are thinking. You want to stay there?"

Mike laughed. "It's perfect. Yau's goons are never going to look *right there!*"

"Where?" Karen and Jia said it at the same time. And then the coin dropped. "What?" "Are you crazy?" "...no way!"

Karen took a step closer to look into Dean's eyes. "We saw... something in the pictures from that attic. What did it look like to you?"

Dean shrugged. "I don't know. It..." He sighed. "It was strange. I felt like in a trance – suddenly I seemed to be so far away from myself. I was suddenly in a childhood memory. Maybe the air was really bad down there, or something. And the shadows – well, there were shadows in those dust clouds. But what does that mean?"

He reached out and hugged Karen. She gave him a light kiss on his dirty cheek. Then she pushed him back. "You'll have to take a shower if you want me to kiss you again, sailor."

Dean turned around with a smile and went to the guest bathroom. When he had closed the door, Mike turned to the women. "I was sitting on the roof when it happened. Suddenly I saw myself... sitting there. Like Dean I felt like I had left my body. I had never felt anything like that!"

Karen shivered and whispered to herself. "That's what my grandfather said in the letter - it is haunted gold."

LATER THAT NIGHT they ordered food from the hotel next door. Shanghai was still the only place in China were this kind of 24-hour service was common. A short while later several hamburgers and fish and chips arrived at their apartment. They ate with gusto. Dean could not remember ever having been so hungry. The climbing and the tension of the evening had taken a lot out of him.

They were trying to keep the conversation light and nobody was even looking at the two bundles they had looted from the attic.

"So Mike, your family lives in San Francisco?"

"Yeah. My dad was in the army and had been stationed for the longest time in the Presidio. I remember as a child we had been living for a few years in Alaska, but it's all rather foggy in my mind. We moved to San Francisco when I was five. I was living there until I came here three, no, four years ago." He bit into his hamburger.

"Only child?"

"Mhh-hmm." He swallowed. "Yes. And you?"

Karen wiped her hands on a napkin. The fish and chips were great. "One younger brother. He's also living in Chicago. So your parents must be missing you, so far away."

"Yeah. They do. It's kinda tough, but this is a great job and now that I am together with Jia... we may move back to the States later, but for know this here is our home. I think my parents understand. My father actually encouraged me to take the job. He said 'You are young and young people should see the world. It's the only thing that can save us from ourselves.'"

"Wise words." Karen lifted her beer bottle and they all brought their bottles and glasses together and drank.

THEY WENT TO bed around 3am, too exhausted to open the Tyvek rolls. They just left it all in the living room and retired to their rooms.

Dean switched off the light and joined Karen under the warm cover of the bed in the guest room. They held each other tight and kissed, reveling in the warmth of their bodies.

MIKE WAS WORKING his way through an enormous omelette. With his fork he pointed at the bundles they had brought from the hotel the night before.

"So after we've been checking out this stuff, we start packing and we go to the Suzhou Hotel. I've heard they have started to modernize some of the rooms and that there are now a few pretty nice suites up on the fifth floor in the back of the building."

Dean got up after he was done with his cereal and brought his backpack from last night over to the others. He reached in the bag and put the gold bars on the table, one after another. The metal had an almost creamy golden shine under the morning light.

THEY ALL STARED at the bars, their faces a mix of fear and fascination.

Karen took one of the bars, surprised by its weight and the sheer feeling of density that came off it. "These are heavy!"

The metal felt slightly soft to the skin. She held the bar up in front of her face and turned it slowly. All the others' eyes had been following her movements.

The bars had rounded corners and their surface was not completely smooth. There were tiny dimples in the material, as if the cast had not been of a high quality. They had been produced in wartime China, probably in a rush.

A small seal had been stamped into one side of the bar. Light was glittering off the complex Chinese characters embossed in the gold:

時間的監護人

Karen pointed at the seal and turned to Jia. "Can you read these characters?"

"Good question. They are traditional Chinese characters, not the modernized versions we use here nowadays, and it doesn't seem to be common words." Jia took another one of the bars and took a close look at the characters. With her other hand she was writing the different strokes of the characters into thin air in front of her. Her mouth moved silently in concentration.

"Maybe..." Her right eyebrow moved up. "It could be the name of a company – an approximate translation would be 'Guardians of Time'."

"Sounds like the name of an insurance company to me." Mike also had taken one of the bars. "So one of these bars is worth about fifteen thousand dollars, hm?" He moved his hand up and down, judging the mass of the bar.

"LET'S SEE WHAT else we've got." He put the gold down and walked over to the two bundles they had dropped off next to the entrance.

He knelt down and unwrapped the first bundle. It was the three long boxes, very light, made from thin boards. One of the long sides had obviously been the lid that had been screwed shut at the end. Two screws on each end of the box had to be undone. Mike took a power tool from his toolbox and went to work. The screws had been sitting in the wood for half a century and he had to use quite some force to get them to move. But once the power tool was turning, it was a matter of seconds for each screw to be free of the lid.

Mike pulled the lid off the box and for a while just sat there. The three others had come over and were now standing around him. Then Mike gingerly hooked his index fingers on both sides into a rolled up document and lifted it straight up out of the box. He held it high and stood up. Jia knelt down before him and slowly pulled down the edge of the roll. It was very rough, heavy paper that had taken on the rolled up shape permanently through the long time it had been stored in the box.

THE SCROLL WAS maybe two feet wide and five feet long. It was the most exquisite Chinese calligraphy. Fine lines danced across the paper, creating a large Chinese character in the middle of the paper out of hundreds of lines of small writing. Even for Karen and Dean, who had not much experience with Asian calligraphy, it was a breathtaking piece of art.

Jia was trying to read at least a part of the text. "It is – or at least I think it is – a philosophical text. It talks a lot about how life and time are actually not separate things... It is written almost like a speech or a prayer or something."

Dean behind her had started to take pictures of the piece. "Do you think this would be of interest nowadays? It's hard for me to judge if we've actually stumbled over invaluable pieces of art or just some guy's old calligraphy collection."

Jia nodded. "I think this is very valuable. I have never seen calligraphy like this. I think this scroll is very, very old. But the text is... strange." She kept on looking at the scroll, captivated by the half-understood text. Finally she had to shake her head to free herself from it and she slowly let go. The scroll rolled itself back into the small tube of stiff paper that they had started with, only slightly more loose than before.

Mike and Dean slowly maneuvered the text back into the box, but they only loosely closed the lid. They unrolled the other Tyvek bundle and took out the two small boxes that Dean had chosen randomly from one of the stacks. Both boxes were cubes, five inches along the edges. These also had one side that had been screwed shut during the packing process, and Dean held one of the boxes for Mike to use his power tool on. The lid came off after only a few seconds.

KAREN LOOKED INTO the box and gasped. She slowly moved her hand into the box and gingerly removed a sphere from the red silk padding. She held the sphere up into the light and it glittered.

"Look at this!"

It was a sphere of gold, about three inches in diameter and a wall thickness of not more than an eighth of an inch, with dozens of large holes in sinuous shapes revealing another golden sphere inside, which again had holes that revealed another smaller sphere inside, and so on.

Altogether five spheres were visible. The spheres shared an axis that connected them and they all moved quite freely. Karen pushed the second sphere through one of the holes, and it rotated slowly for some time before coming to rest again. Karen shivered involuntarily as if cold air was pouring out of the sphere in her hands.

The curved outside surface of each sphere was decorated with a pattern that looked almost like Chinese characters, but they were different. Many of the strokes that made up an individual character never connected. The strokes were mostly in parallel or they were not long enough to cross each other.

All the others had been staring at the golden sphere, but nobody said a word.

Karen slowly lowered the sphere back into the box. She looked at Jia. "Now I may not know much about China and Chinese culture, but this doesn't look like the usual historical artifacts."

"Yes, you are right. I'm also not an expert, but I have never seen anything like this!"

Mike and Dean had already been working on opening the other box. When the lid came off, Dean dropped it to the side and reached in the box. Another set of spheres appeared in his hand, but with this one the outer shell had one larger opening on one side.

Karen was fascinated by the sphere. "They are beautiful. It looks like the gold has a mirror finish."

DEAN USED THE palm of his hand to spin the inner sphere, faster this time than when Karen had done so before. It rotated almost effortlessly, and a low humming sound made all the hairs on their arms stand up. Dean's eyes turned wide. His arm and hand holding the sphere felt like frozen, he did not have any control over them. Goosebumps raced up and down his body and his eyesight narrowed until he could only see the golden sphere sparkle in the light.

Jia was standing close to Dean, and it felt like waves of cold and heat were churning through her body. She felt like she was falling towards Dean, but at the same time her feet never left the ground. She saw Dean turning gray, like all color had been sucked into the sphere. The sphere glittered, and there was also a deep inner glow to it.

Mike wanted to reach out to Dean, but like on the roof of the hotel when he had been watching Dean on the laptop, everything seemed to slow down. He felt cold and dizzy. He heard some sort of loud crack behind him over the hum of the sphere. The glittering light of the sphere was unnaturally bright.

It was coming from *inside* the sphere. He tried to talk, but he was too confused to string coherent words together. "Deeeeee..."

Karen had been kneeling on the ground when Dean spun up the sphere. It seemed that the floor under her legs was bending towards Dean. Her stomach lifted like in a roller coaster. Her hair turned electric and stood up, towards Dean. The hum of the sphere sounded like a hundred men's voices singing a flat note in a very sad key.

"...eaaaann!"

IT WAS ALL over in less than twenty seconds. Dean dropped the sphere and it bounced off the carpet with a heavy thump. Dean collapsed, but immediately regained consciousness when he dropped to the the floor, his head hitting the golden sphere.

Karen lunged forward. "Dean! Dean!" She landed on her stomach next to Dean's crumpled body. "Are you alright?"

Jia went down on her knees. Mike stepped forward to hold her by the shoulders.

"What was that!" Dean felt like he had cotton in his mouth. He was dizzy and his stomach felt sick. He looked at Karen and he had trouble focusing on her face. "Oh. Karen... are you OK?"

She laughed hoarsely. "Am I OK? Me? I don't know what this thing just did, but you are the one who was holding it!" She touched his face. His skin was cold to the touch.

She helped Dean up and together with Mike they managed to get Dean to sit down on the sofa. His steps were unsteady and he was as dizzy as if he had been spinning like a top for several minutes.

JIA HAD GONE to the kitchen to heat some water for tea and when she came out of the kitchen, she carefully picked the golden sphere from the carpet. It felt very warm to the touch. It had engravings on the surfaces of all the inner spheres like the first one they had examined, again the same strange characters that looked like Chinese, but weren't. She slowly dropped it back into its cage made of red silk and wood.

"Oh! Look!" She pointed at the window. There was a long crack along the top of the window, essentially cutting one corner off from the rest of the pane. Mike saw it, too. "Yeah – I remember hearing that! The window cracked when the sphere was spinning."

"But what happened?" Dean was trying to understand. "I spun up the inner sphere, and suddenly it felt like I got sucked into it, as if everything around me was changing. It felt like time was slowing down around me."

"Yes! Me too."

"Same here."

"And the floor was bending towards you."

"Yes, I also thought I was leaning towards you, but I wasn't really moving. It was scary. Oh – and everything changed colors somehow, and the sphere was glowing!"

Mike looked at Dean. "Guardians of Time, eh?"

Dean cleared his throat. "Yeah. That translation is starting to make a lot more sense now. Does anybody have any clue what the hell those spheres do? My physics teacher never mentioned anything like *that*."

JIA HAD BROUGHT some tea and Dean leaned back on the sofa and inhaled the smell of the jasmine tea.

Mike looked back at the cracked window and then back at his friends. "Is that why Yau is so interested in his old boxes? He must have known what's in there. I mean, he is stinking rich. So even if it would be tens of millions of dollars worth of gold, that doesn't sound like it would be worth an old man's time. But these spheres... and remember we have a roomful of boxes. This is just the tip of the iceberg!"

They all looked at each other. Mike spoke again. "OK, first of all, let's get the hell out of here. Yau's men know we live here and they are obviously keeping this building under observation. It seems they still haven't figured out that we can leave the building around the corner through the hotel, and we should use that. Let's pack."

29

JIA AND MIKE had taken their two cars out of the garage, driving around the block several times and spotting each other to see if they were followed. Then Mike turned east towards the Bund, while Jia picked up Karen and Dean at the entrance of the hotel.

When their little red car left the hotel driveway and hopped down the curb onto the road, a man in an orange robe quietly came out of the shadows of the lobby and got into the back of a waiting black Volkswagen with tinted windows. The black car rolled silently down the driveway and turned in the same direction as Jia's car.

JIA PARKED THE car across the street of the hotel with two wheels on the sidewalk. Her fast and reckless driving style had left Karen and Dean even more shaken after their already quite interesting morning. They pulled their bags from the car when Mike came out of the hotel.

"It's about time you arrive! I've got us two suites over on the east side on the fifth floor. I've taken a look and they are quite nice. And we have a connecting door!" He took two of the bags from Jia and guided them into the hotel.

"About time?" Dean was shifting the weight of his travel bag. "You do know that Jia drives like she's possessed by demons, don't you? We couldn't have been here faster with a helicopter."

THEIR ROOMS WERE big. Each suite consisted of a bedroom, bathroom and small living area. The living areas of the two suites were connected with a door. The rooms had their original dark red wood paneling which had recently been cleaned and the walls had been freshly painted. The bathrooms had been completely replaced and were modern with jacuzzi baths and bright lights.

After settling down in their fourth room in a week, Karen and Dean came over to the other living room and found their friends in front of Mike's laptop.

"WE'VE BEEN DOING some googling. There's nothing at all out on the Web about some sort of guardians of time, especially some with an apparent gold fetish."

"Do you know anybody here in town who could help us?" Karen sat down next to them. Dean walked over to the window and looked out at one of the new huge bridges that connected the old Shanghai with the new commercial areas across the river.

Mike was passing his hands through his hair, looking up at the ceiling. "Not really. Most of my foreign friends are engineers – and most of the Chinese friends I have are my colleagues. Well... there is one person I can think of." He looked at Jia. "I wonder if Helen is in town. In summer she sometimes goes off to the north."

Jia's eyes were lighting up. "Helen! That is a great idea. And I know she is still here - I saw her just last week in the café out at the campus."

Dean turned from the window. "Who is Helen?"

"Her name is Helen Turner. She has been living in Shanghai and Hong Kong all her life and she is now in her late seventies. She's a legend around here with the expats. She knows everybody and she writes articles about the local history for magazines and has published several books. Let me call her up and see if she has time."

MIKE TOOK OUT his cell phone, looked up her name and dialed.

"Oh – Hi Helen! How are you? This is Mike Moritaka." He held his free hand out with the thumb up. "Yeah, I know... we should have gone out for dinner sometime. You know how it is with young lovers." He laughed and kissed Jia on the forehead. She pouted at him. "Yes. I know. Listen, Helen, I have a bit of a problem where I need your encyclopedic knowledge of Chinese and Shanghai history." He was listening and playing with Jia's hair who took his hand and twisted it. "No, I can't really tell you on the phone... it is rather delicate. Can I come by this afternoon with some friends and talk to you about it? Really? OK." He untwisted his arm from Jia's grasp and looked at his watch. "See you in an hour! Bye!"

Mike looked at them. "We are lucky! We have one hour to get across town, so we should probably leave."

They decided to bring along the first sphere they had taken out of the boxes. They carefully put the box with the sphere nestled in red silk into a small backpack.

They took Mike's little red car since it was by far less identifiable. Mike explained. "In fact, it looks exactly like some ten thousand taxis all around us. Nobody is able to follow this car through town."

When they joined the stream of cars going across the steel bridge at the mouth of Suzhou Creek, a black Volkswagen started its engine and slowly followed them across the bridge.

30

HELEN TURNER WAS a small woman with a round, surprisingly youthful face surrounded by curly, light gray hair. Her skin was slightly tanned and clear with only a few wrinkles around the eyes. She looked like everybody's favorite grandmother.

She was sitting in a comfortable study on the ground floor of her French-colonial townhouse in one of the few untouched neighborhoods of Shanghai. The room had a large window facing a small garden with lush green trees, the rest of the walls were covered with shelves holding thousands of books. A small air conditioner built into one corner of the window was fighting a losing battle against the humidity and heat.

Helen's secretary, a young Chinese woman in a business suit and steel rimmed glasses, had shown the four friends into the room.

"Ah – Jia and Mike! What a beautiful couple! If this is the future of humankind, I think we still have a chance at this game... and who are your friends?" Helen looked squarely at Dean and Karen, and it seemed to Dean she was not missing the smallest detail about them.

"Hi Helen! You look as beautiful as ever yourself! This is Karen Chadbourne and Dean Lashure."

Helen held out her hand and both Karen and Dean shook hands with her.

"Nice to meet you!" She pointed at the laptop on her desk. "I'm wasting my time writing up another long book about Shanghai's history... sometimes I get the feeling I'm the only one still interested in these things."

"Oh no. That's not true! I know for a fact that your last book is selling very well overseas. You are the talk of town, you know." Mike smiled at her sweetly.

"Ah... old-fashioned charm. Nice to know they still make that." She laughed and wiggled a finger at Mike. She looked at all of them and pointed at a couple of chairs and a sofa. "Where are my manners... Please sit down."

"So, as I've said, we have a problem where you may be able to help..."

Mike stopped as the door had opened. Helen's assistant pushed the door with her back, carrying a tray with tea. She sat it down on a small side table and gave Helen a questioning look.

"That is all, Joy. I won't need you for this meeting."

The assistant nodded without a word and left the room, softly closing the door behind herself.

HELEN LOOKED BACK at Mike. "Yes, your phone call was very mysterious. What is it that you can't discuss on a phone system, that, as I remember, you are helping to construct?"

"Very funny." Mike turned to Dean who opened the backpack so that Mike could pull the box out. He opened the box carefully and slowly lifted the sphere out of the silk padding. Its polished surface caught the light from the window and the curved edges of the holes in the outer sphere glittered like a diamond made of gold. All the eyes in the room focused on the sphere.

Helen gasped. "Oh! It's beautiful!"

"We would like to know if you have ever seen one of these or if you have any references to spheres like this in your library." He slowly handed her the sphere and said. "Be careful. It's hard to explain why, but try not to spin the inner spheres."

Helen nodded and took the sphere and inspected the engraved characters on the surface with a magnifying glass from her desk. It was completely silent in the room with four people holding their breath and only quiet ticking noises from Helen's laptop as its little hard disk spun.

"Hmm." Helen Turner put the magnifying glass back on her desk and slowly rolled the sphere in her hand. "Where did you get this?"

"We can't really tell you right now. Mostly because it seems that everybody who gets involved with this thing gets into trouble with some very unsavory characters. I don't want you to get pulled into this."

"I'm asking because until a few minutes ago I would have sworn on a stack of bibles that these things were part of a fairy tale!" She held the sphere up. The four friend's eyes followed it like a dog's eyes follow a tennis ball.

HELEN HELD THE sphere with both hands on her lap. She looked at them. "Well, well. I will have to check some old books, but I actually remember hearing about these myself." Her eyes had a faraway look.

"It was in 1943. I was on board of the Leicester, a small passenger ship on the way from Shanghai to Sydney. The Japanese had let go of about 300 interned British nationals and we had been sent off on this ship to Australia. I hated leaving Shanghai. It was my home, I had never been so far away from it before. But my mother was happy to get away and after we arrived in Sydney, she would never again leave Australia."

"It was a colorful group of people, more than 250 women and children and about fifty men. I was in love with one of the men. His name was Geoffrey. He was a journalist for one of the newspapers here in Shanghai and he was at the time 22 years old and beautiful, oh so beautiful. I loved him like only a thirteen year old girl can love a man. And he would never know about it."

HELEN TOOK ONE of the beautiful Chinese porcelain cups that her assistant had brought in. She sipped the hot tea and continued. "In the evenings I often talked to Geoffrey out on deck. He always stood at the stern, looking back the way we had come, smoking his strong cigarettes. He told me stories about Shanghai. I think he loved the city even more than I did, and I was the only one on the Leicester who was not completely sick of the place. So he told me stories, some so beautiful and exotic that I believed he made them up for me."

Helen's audience of four was captivated by her description. Other than an occasional slurp of tea nothing but her voice could be heard.

"One of his stories was about the Guardians of Time."

That got a reaction. Jia had just been drinking tea and started to cough. They all pulled in air. Helen didn't seem to notice or care. She was gazing at the books behind the four friends and kept on talking.

"Geoffrey had been writing a story about some of the more prominent gangsters in Shanghai, and it was pretty easy to get invited to their houses. You have to understand, these people were part of high society." She laughed to herself. "That's the kind of town Shanghai was. To be someone, you had to be born white, or you had to be a career criminal too dangerous to arrest."

"One day Geoffrey had been in the house of Martin Yau. I've actually met Mr. Yau several times in Hong Kong later on. So Geoffrey was in Yau's house on a weekend for Tiffin as we called a good brunch back then, and it was a rainy Saturday, so nobody wanted to leave. Tiffin turned into tea, which turned into dinner. Everybody was pretty drunk by then, and Yau had become talkative."

"And talking is what he did. He told the group about the mountain villages he had inherited, somewhere in central China. His father had been a warlord out there – I think in Hunan somewhere - and had just recently been killed in fights with the communists. The communists had to flee after ransacking the area for food and a quick re-education campaign, and it had all fallen in Yau's hands – a whole area with all the people and everything, villages, mountains, the whole lot!"

"Yau said that he had found an empty temple complex near one of the villages. The communists had seemingly killed most of the monks, but they had to run before setting fire to the buildings. And Yau found these buildings to be full of treasure. There was gold and documents and ancient Chinese art and rooms full of... golden spheres!" Helen again lifted the sphere in her hands.

"Yau called the monks 'Guardians of Time', but he never explained why. He said he was spending good money on figuring out what the spheres were for and that he was now bringing everything to Shanghai so that he could get scholars in the city to take a look. And then he went to another room and brought back a golden sphere. Geoffrey told me exactly what it looked like – he said he had been holding it for a moment. It was very much like this one. It could be this very sphere he was holding all those years ago." Her voice had become a whisper. She looked closely at the sphere and slowly turned it in her hands, her mind on a first love, long lost.

AFTER A LITTLE while she sighed and handed the sphere back to Mike with a wistful smile. "I'm an old nostalgic, in case you haven't noticed."

Jia sniffed. She had been silently crying. She wiped her eyes and shrugged. "Love stories!" She shook her head.

Mike looked back at Helen. "Do you know anything about these markings on the sphere? It does look very similar to Chinese characters, but I'm not even sure if these are actually writing or just some sort of decoration."

"I noticed them, indeed. Very round and fluid with lots of parallels. They are actually very similar to old Chinese characters found on bronze vessels from around 1000BC. But these are very strange. The strokes do not connect. I have some friends here in the University that I can ask about this. I will not tell them where I saw it, they are used to me asking them strange questions."

"NOW, WHILE I understand why you are reluctant to talk about this... if this is in any way connected to Martin Yau, I have to warn you."

She had their full attention.

"This man is incredibly dangerous. As you know, Mike, I've been living in Hong Kong for more than 30 years and I've actually met Yau on several occasions socially."

She took another sip from her tea.

"How old is he now? Ninety? He probably still runs circles around the younger gang bosses down there. He has survived the most aggressive and bitter gang wars you can imagine for over fifty years now, which is something that can not be said about his opponents. If there is anything he is really good at, it is being angry at people for no good reason. He is a vindictive, murderous son of a bitch if there ever was one."

The words sounded strange out of the mouth of this little old lady. But her voice was cold as steel. Listening to her, Karen had a sinking feeling in her stomach. After all, she had now twice been aggressively fighting Yau's men. It did not sound as if Yau would forget about that.

"So there you have it. Any other questions?"

DEAN CLEARED HIS throat. "Did you ever hear anything else about these Guardians of Time?"

"No, not that I can remember. Assuming that Martin Yau told the truth back when he talked to Geoffrey, it is possible that the monastery never reopened. After all, less than ten years later the Communists took over China, and they had a pretty low opinion of religious groups. They disbanded virtually all the monasteries in central and eastern China."

Helen pointed at the bookshelves. "I'll take a look and see if I can find any mention of the Guardians of Time. And maybe I can at least figure out where the land of Yau's father was located. That should give us a clue as to where we can find the temple he was talking about. I'll call you if I find something."

They took their cue and got up, thanking Helen for her time. She saw them to the door. "It so nice seeing you again. Jia, take care of Mike – he seems to always get into trouble, doesn't he? And it was really nice meeting you." She again shook hands with Karen and Dean.

THEY STOOD IN a small circle under the trees in front of Helen Turner's house. It was a quiet side street, lined with trees and just a few cars and motor scooters passing by. The sidewalks were buckled and twisted by tree roots and looked like they had not been repaired since colonial times. Most of the houses were like Helen's, small townhouses in a distinctly Parisian style, that once housed officials of the French settlement in Shanghai and their families. The shadow of the trees made it an acceptable place for an impromptu meeting.

MIKE ABSENTMINDEDLY KICKED a root that was arching out of the pavement in front of his feet. He was looking down, thinking hard. "So what are we going to do?"

Dean was looking at Karen. "Well, we don't have much of a choice. We can try and contact Yau and tell him where his loot is. I'm sure he'd be happy about that, but the more I hear about him I suspect we would still end up dead. After all, he knows everything about us and he obviously has no problems with sending his hired help after us, wherever we are."

"And then we can try and recover the artwork and gold ourselves. We still have then several options on what to do with it. Either we keep the gold or not, and I'm not sure how hard that would be to pull off since we are in China, after all. Keeping the gold has the advantage of leveling the playing field a little bit – we are still in trouble with Yau, but at least we have some funds."

"As far as the artwork is concerned, I'd say we anonymously drop it all off at the local museum. I don't want to rob the Chinese off their heritage. And then somebody else can try and figure out what these golden spheres do."

Karen nodded. "I like the idea about the artwork. With the gold... I don't know. If we give it to anybody but Yau, he's going to come after us. So yeah... I agree. We should probably hang on to the gold bars and see if we can use it as leverage."

Jia looked back and forward between the two. "I think so, too. And I'm sure I can help with liquidating the gold. A lot of Chinese buy gold as an investment."

Mike finally looked up. "Great. My girlfriend, the fence." He laughed. "We still assume that Yau wants to get the gold. What if he knows – or thinks he knows - what the spheres are for?"

Dean shrugged. "Well, I'm for sure not handing the spheres over to some crime lord. That stuff should be investigated in a laboratory somewhere."

Mike nodded. "So I guess that's decided. The artwork will be donated to the Shanghai museum, no matter what!" He smiled mischievously. "And we'll decide about the gold once we see what the market can carry."

"It's now three. We can't really do anything until later tonight. Karen and I are going to walk around a bit." Dean took Karen's hand.

"Ah... young love!" Mike rolled his eyes. "OK then, see you later." He hugged Jia and the two went to where they had parked the car. Mike was carrying the backpack with the sphere on one shoulder.

DEAN LED KAREN through a densely populated area of Shanghai, and after a leisurely half-hour walk they entered a busy street market with a temple, a large fishpond and a teahouse in its center.

Dean shook his head. "Just in case you have been wondering, I was really lost." Karen laughed at him. She had been wondering about that. "But this I recognize, I have been here last time I was in Shanghai. This is the Yu Yuan temple."

They bought some steamed dumplings from a street vendor, got two tickets for the temple grounds and went for a walk through the extensive temple garden.

THEY WERE SITTING on a bench in a shadowy corner of the garden, eating their dumplings. Karen leaned back and sighed. "Finally alone. It's so hard in China to be away from other people." She leaned over and kissed Dean on the cheek.

He turned to her and kissed her back. Then he looked out at the little rock garden behind one of the temple buildings. A monk in an orange robe was standing on the other side of the rock formation, watching it, deep in thought.

Dean leaned back, shoulder to shoulder with Karen. "It's been a busy week. I hope we can resolve this one way or another. We won't be able to run away forever."

She was watching his face in profile. He had stopped shaving and he had now a stubbly chin. His beard would be a lot lighter than his brown hair, and it seemed to come out in uneven colors. She smiled. "You look tired. I don't know how I will ever be able to thank you for all this. You could as well just have left me sitting there in the hotel in San Francisco."

"Yeah... it sure has been a lesson about developing other people's old film." He scratched his stubbly chin and turned back to her.

She held up a hand and stroked his face, the beard tickling her fingers. She pulled his head closer and they kissed again.

IN HER PERIPHERAL vision, Karen saw a orange shape moving closer. They broke their kiss and turned to the garden, where the monk was now blocking the view of the weathered rocks. She was hoping they had not broken some sort of temple rule with their teenage behavior. She was about to say something, when the man started to speak.

"Excuse me for interrupting." His English was fluent. His face was not showing any emotion, and the dark orange hood was shadowing his expressions even further. He was tall and had a narrow, ascetic face with dark brown skin and black eyes. His skin looked like he had spent all his life outdoors. He reminded Karen of photos she had seen of Nepalese and Tibetan monks.

Both Dean and Karen stared at him with interest.

"It is most improper for me to speak to you without introduction." He bent his back slightly in a symbolic bow to them. "But it is of the utmost importance that I do so."

Dean slowly became uncomfortable with this situation. While the man did not look like he was working for Yau, how could they know? "Who are you?"

The man came a little closer to where they were sitting. He held out his hands, palms forward. "I am not here to threaten you! My... associates and I assume that you may have something that originally belonged to our organization."

Dean was not feeling better yet. "Funny, I've heard this before, not so long ago."

"This is no laughing matter, Mr. Lashure."

Dean looked at him openmouthed. Then he turned to Karen. "Does everybody now know our names?"

HE TURNED BACK to the monk. "How do you know who I am?"

"Oh, we have been following you since we felt that somebody had found our... objects of art?"

"Sorry, but you must be mistaken. I'm not in the art business." Something that the man had just said was bothering Dean. Something was wrong.

Karen cleared her throat. "How do you know you are talking to the right people? What if we just deny anything you say?"

"Oh, we *know*. It is not something you could hide from us. We've been waiting for many years for the signs..."

Dean finally had it. He interrupted the monk. "Did you say you *felt* that somebody found your objects?"

The monk focused on him and bowed again slightly. "Yes. We know that you have access to something we own. There is no denying it!"

"You said you have been waiting for many years?" Karen asked.

Now the man bowed to her. "Yes. We have been waiting for almost sixty years. We knew that someday we would see the signs and that our mission was not in vain."

"You are one of the Guardians of Time?" Karen was incredulous.

The man took a few moments before he answered.

"Yes."

KAREN AND DEAN looked at each other. They both saw questions piling up behind each other's eyes. Dean was the first to turn back to the monk. "First of all, how can we believe you? We will have to see some sort of proof." He realized that this was a pretty dumb thing to say. What proof could the man possibly have that he would even understand?

But the monk nodded and pulled his robe back. His hood fell down and revealed a shaved head that shone in the sun like a billiard ball. He pulled further and revealed his surprisingly muscular breast. A large round tattoo filled his breast from shoulder to shoulder and neck to breastbone. It were several Chinese characters in a circle, tattooed in black ink. Karen and Dean couldn't read the words, but they didn't have to. It was obviously the same seal as the one on the gold bars.

The monk silently closed his robe and pulled the hood back over his head. Dean was impressed with how completely composed and calm the man had been up to now, with no emotion whatsoever escaping his features.

"We may be able to help you. But there are... complications. There are other people who are interested in what we found."

The monk nodded. "I understand. We have been dealing with Martin Yau and his father before him for a long time. You are in danger."

"It would help if we would know more about the -" He heard a short, controlled sound like a small balloon exploding just behind his head. The monk jerked back and his hood slipped from his head. A look of utter shock and surprise was the first – and last - emotion Dean would see on his face. A small hole in his robe started to grow into a red circle.

KAREN GASPED AND held a hand to her mouth. Her eyes were big in shock. Dean jumped up and turned to the sound. A man in a dark blue suit sprayed something into his face. He saw Karen jump towards him, but suddenly there was a fist appearing in his field of vision, hitting Karen hard at the temple. More spray everywhere. It was stinging in his eyes and his vision became blurry.

He tried to hold his breath and to step forward and catch Karen, but his legs did not react to his commands, his knees were becoming weak. Something hit him in the neck. He saw gravel and dirt close up. His face hurt.

Everything turned to darkness.

31

WET. SOMETHING WET. Water was splashing into his face! Dean opened his eyes to see the underside of a car seat. There was something in his mouth... small stones. Gravel. His back hurt. His head hurt. He started spitting. Got to get rid of the gravel. He was spitting blood and little stones onto a dark blue carpet.

"He's waking up." A voice, very close.

The car engine was slowing down. Somebody was reaching over him, opening the car door next to his head. He tried to look around, but he couldn't move his arms, they were tied together behind his back.

More water was hitting his head. He heard an empty water bottle fall onto the road just outside of the car. Suddenly his arms were free. He tried to move, but the person sitting over him took his left arm and right shoulder and lifted him up.

"Whaaaa!" He was falling forward. He was able to push his right arm in front of his head, hot flashes of pain shooting through the wrist as he hit the asphalt. He rolled on his side, more pain in the arm, and he got his first good look of the car. Red twilight filled the sky.

THE MAN IN the backseat was moving over to where Dean had been lying, and leaned out of the car to pull the door shut. He paused and looked at Dean. The last reflections of an already sunken sun glinted off his dark sunglasses.

"Listen. We have Chadbourne and we will do whatever necessary to make you comply with our demands. Understood?"

Dean nodded, screaming pain was shooting through his neck.

"Good. We will call you on this." A black cell phone bounced off Dean's shoulder and landed in front of him on the ground, slowly spinning to a stop.

The car door snapped shut and the black limousine left with a protesting squeak from its tires. Dean dropped his head to the ground, closing his eyes.

No! He could not let go. Karen was in danger. He slowly pushed himself up on all fours. He got up, dizzy, exhausted, hurting. He almost went down again when he picked up the cell phone. A DynaRola. Of course. Fate enjoyed little jokes like that.

Dean looked around unsteadily. The sun had sunk just behind a large suspension bridge with tall towers. He knew that bridge, he remembered seeing it from the Suzhou Hotel. With a heading for the sinking sun and the bridge he had a good idea of were he was. It was probably a walk of two or three miles back to the hotel, but that would give him a chance to make plans.

KAREN HEARD THE noise of a loud air-conditioner. No. It was more than that. The room was moving. It was a jet! She was in a small jet and the engine had just revved up.

She was trying to blink her eyes back to seeing, but it didn't work. She was blindfolded. Her hands had been tied in front of her with something soft, maybe a strip of cloth. Karen was trying to take stock of her situation, but there were too many unknowns.

She suddenly remembered the last moments in the Yu Yuan garden. Dean! She still saw his look of determination, trying to reach her. But there was this... gas everywhere. Her last memory was of falling down. Falling, falling.

Then another jolt. The monk! He had been shot, right there, in front of her. She remembered the blood spreading on his orange robe, just where she had seen his tattoo.

Karen heard voices, but it was too far away to understand anything. Two men were laughing. A door was falling shut. The cockpit door? Somebody came back to her seat and was checking her seatbelt and the cloth tied around her wrists. She smelled aftershave.

THE MAN SAT down next to her. "Good evening, Miss Chadbourne. I'm sorry for the blindfold, but you have instilled quite a lot of respect in some of our men. Just lean back and enjoy the flight." His voice was very smooth, with a strong British accent. If he was from Hong Kong, he must have gone to schools in Britain.

"Who are you? Where are we going?" She felt panic rise in her heart.

"My name is of no consequence to you. And it is going to be a flight of about one hour."

Hong Kong. It had to be Hong Kong. The time was off, but why should he tell her the accurate flight time. It's not like she could ask for her money back. Despite herself she had to smile. This was the kind of thing Dean would have said. She missed him. With Dean she had been fearless, not because she thought that he would come to her rescue with guns blazing, but because she felt that together they were larger than the sum of the parts. Now she was flying away from him at close to the speed of sound.

32

DEAN OPENED THE door to his suite and knocked on the connecting door, not even bothering to switch on a light. He could hear voices and music on the other side and steps coming his way.

The door opened and there was music and light and warmth and friends and... Dean stumbled forward.

"Woah! What happened?" Mike caught him and pulled him over to the bed. Dean sat down heavily. He had to use his arms to keep himself upright.

Jia had been sitting at a small desk next to the window with Mike's notebook computer. Now she stood up, turned down the sound of the TV with a swift motion and came over. "Oh Dean! You look horrible!" She looked through the connecting door at the dark room on the other side. She turned back at Dean, now alarmed. "And where is Karen?"

Jia took a closer look at Dean and his bloodied face and turned around. She walked over to the bathroom and got a small first-aid kit from her cosmetic case.

"They got Karen." Dean felt like crying. This was not at all going well. They had ignored all warning signs and now they would have to pay the price. He sighed deeply.

"When did that happen?" Mike was kneeling in front of him, watching Jia clean out several deep scratches on his cheek and forehead.

"Maybe two hours ago. We were in the Yu Yuan Garden – you know, the temple? And these guys came, shot the monk we were talking to and knocked us out with some gas. Ouch!" Jia had jerked and touched a nasty gash on his forehead. She stepped back and stared at him.

Mike had been rolling backwards and was now leaning back on his arms. He looked incredulous. "Did you say they shot one of the monks in the Yu Yuan Temple? A monk? They shot a monk?"

Dean closed his eyes. His skin looked unnaturally white in the gloom of the two bedside lamps. "The monk was not from the temple. He was one of the Guardians of Time."

"What?" Shouted both Jia and Mike.

DEAN STARTED TO tell the story from the beginning, interrupted by vocal explosions at the high points.

"...and then he opened his robe and showed us a tattoo on his breast and it was the same as the embossed seal on those damn gold bars!" "No way!"

"...they shot him. Point-blank..." "Oh my god!"

"...kicked me out of the car!" "But where was Karen?" "I have no idea!"

"...gave me a cell phone. They'd call, he said."

Mike looked up. "They gave you a cell phone? Let me see!" He stretched out his hand and Dean dropped the black DynaRola phone into it.

MIKE LOOKED AT it from all sides, slid open the back and closed it again and then switched it on. "Very clever. They glued the PIN card into the back with some cyano-acrylic crap.

And they broke the display, so that you can make and receive calls, but there's no way to see any numbers. I'm sure they also used one of the hacks from the Internet to permanently scramble the ID code sent to the cell phone towers." He flipped it over and over in his hand. "Well I guess it's working. The little green LED up here..." He pointed at it with his index finger. "- when it blinks from time to time like... right now! That means that the cell phone has found one of our towers and is waiting for a call."

He gave it back to Dean. "Listen. When they call, keep them on the line for as long as possible! This is important, OK? Keep them talking for more than thirty seconds and I should be able to trace them or maybe even get their number."

Dean nodded. He was exhausted beyond words. He looked at Jia. "We may need some capital. With Yau going for open war on us, we will have to be able to either fight back or run away really, really fast. Is there a chance to turn some of the gold we have retrieved into money?"

Jia didn't even think for a second. "Sure. I will talk to one of my uncles. He has his own import-export business here in the city, and I know for a fact that he is always frantically trying to get rid of dollars that he 'forgot' to put on his tax returns. He'd invest in anything." She smiled sweetly. "I'll be his favorite niece after this!"

She turned serious again. "I wonder how Karen is doing..."

33

THE PLANE HAD begun to descend a lot faster than she had expected. The mild hum of the engines suddenly turned into an angry roar and wind was buffeting the small jet. Her ears were popping. It was probably a normal descent, but being blindfolded turned it into a new and scary experience.

A sudden thud startled her. They had touched down. The jet was rolling for maybe half a minute when she heard the breaks engage and they stopped. The whine of the engines slowly turned into a low hum and then stopped abruptly.

Karen had been sure that she had just landed in Hong Kong, but when the door opened, the air coming in was cool and smelled like forest. Karen took a deep breath.

The man next to her had not spoken since they left Shanghai. Now he took her left arm and pulled her up. She saw no point in resisting, there had to be other guards close by. For now, following their orders would maybe give her greater freedom than behaving like a caged animal.

"Come with me, Miss Chadbourne." The man pulled her through the door. "Careful. It's four steps down." She slowly navigated the steps and stood on concrete. A light, cool wind blew through her hair and she was glad she had opted for jeans and a long-sleeved shirt in the morning, back in humid Shanghai, a lifetime away already.

There were other men around her, all of them talking in Chinese. The man who had come with her was answering haltingly, and it didn't sound like this was his first or even second language. She noticed that it was otherwise completely quiet. There was wind noises in some trees close by. Where on earth was she? This could surely not be Hong Kong.

They maneuvered her into the backseat of a car, with the man who brought her here sitting to her left again. The driver started the engine without a word and drove off, along bumpy, curvy roads. In films the abducted heroine usually counts street corners and stops and memorizes landmarks by their smell or sound, and Karen was wondering if anybody had ever actually tried that. It did not work for her. Even worse, after a little while she fell asleep.

She woke with a start. It was silent. The engine was ticking lightly as its cooling parts contracted.

"WE ARE HERE. This way Miss Chadbourne." The man took her arm again and pulled her out of the car. He guided her across a single stone step, something she had seen before in Chinese temples. Everything smelled like wood in the cool night air. They walked along a corridor and she heard a door open to her right. A light switch clicked. The man pushed her through the door and turned her around.

"Give me your hands." She stretched her arms out in front of her. The man undid the knot, the cloth fell away from her arms. "Listen. When I close the door, you can remove the blindfold. This is your room. There is a small bathroom and a bed. Don't do anything stupid, there are guards everywhere. The windows are secured with steel bars and the door will be locked. Somebody will bring you food later. Good night." The door fell into the lock in front of her nose. Karen stepped back and pulled the blindfold off her face. She looked around.

THE ROOM WAS twelve by fifteen feet, with a small door on one side and two windows with the curtains drawn. A basic bed with a wooden frame stood on one side under the window. There was a TV! She had a small TV on a stand next to the bathroom door. She went to the bathroom in a hurry. She had to go for quite a while already but had not felt like bringing it up on the plane.

When she came out of the bathroom, she turned the knob on the TV. The volume was set to very low and the volume buttons were missing. There were three channels, all of them in Chinese, and none of them looked like the program was produced anywhere close to Hong Kong. She was still in China.

She was about to fall asleep on the bed when a man unlocked the door. He was Chinese, wearing blue jeans and a white T-Shirt with the words 'HEY LOVELY!' in bold red letters imprinted on his breast. He had a cigarette dangling in the corner of his mouth and he eyed her carefully. Then he slowly pushed a tray into the room with his foot. When the tray cleared the door, he swung it shut and locked it again.

She looked at the food. It was fried rice with egg and various kinds of vegetables in a light blue plastic bowl. There was a fresh pair of throwaway chopsticks on the tray. She broke the chopsticks apart and tried the food - it was actually very good. She started wolfing down the rice while a Chinese soap opera ran behind her. At least they were not starving her to death.

AT ABOUT NINE o'clock in the morning Karen heard the key in the lock turn. The man from last night in the 'HEY LOVELY!' shirt entered the room and held the door open for two more men. One of them was a burly south-east Asian guy in a dark blue suit, black sunglasses, the usual outfit for Yau's men. He was somewhat incongruously carrying a small tray with a bowl of rice, vegetables and some deep-fried bread sticks. He put the breakfast down next to Karen on her bed. She had been sitting on the bed with her arms around her knees, watching Chinese TV.

She now looked at the third man in the room. He was wearing a dark gray suit that by the looks of it must have set him back more than what her car had cost back in Chicago. He was in his mid-forties, muscular, had good looks, and he knew it. His dark eyes were cold as ice. When he was close she noticed an inch-long scar over his right eye.

"GOOD MORNING, MISS Chadbourne. I apologize for having you brought here in the middle of the night like that. But we have some urgent business to discuss." he flashed an insincere smile at her that reminded Karen of a shark smelling blood. She thought that his voice was a touch too high for the role of gangster boss. She did not say anything.

"We know that you and your friends have a number of photos in your possession. In a perfect world, you or Mr. Lashure would have had copies on you when we... took you with us. But not so." He sat down on the edge of the bed, which made it very inconvenient to look at her since Karen was now sitting almost behind him. He got up again and looked unhappy enough to make the Hey-Lovely-guy run out of the room. Seconds later he came back with a white plastic garden chair and placed it behind the man in the gray suit. The man sat down with his elbows on his knees, facing Karen, and sighed as if the weight of the whole world was on his shoulders.

"Now. I would like you to describe the photos to me."

KAREN ALMOST HAD to laugh and it took all her willpower to avoid grinning like mad. It seems that Yau's operation had up to now only succeeded in tracking them to Shanghai and to find where they had been staying until two days ago. She had expected questions about the exact location of the gold, but these people had no idea that they had already found it. She had to be careful about how much to say, but as long as she didn't outright tell them about the attic, they would probably not harm her. Until then she could as well feed them the contents of the photos – with a few strategic holes left here and there.

It took her only about ten minutes to tell the man about the photos. She did not specifically mention the Compton House and she did not talk about the bunched up carpets, the dirt or the rope.

The man's face had become redder as she spoke. He had realized that this was not getting him anything. His voice was louder and shriller when he spoke again.

"That is all?"

"Yes, we've been running around Shanghai for the last few days trying to find the hotel room the pictures had been taken from!" Karen looked at him angrily, which was not very hard for her to do.

"Oh, we know..." He stopped himself and stared at her. He changed direction.

"What did the monk say when you met him in the Yu Yuan Garden?"

She looked at him contemptuously. "The one you shot?"

"Yes!" He jumped up and leaned forward. Before she had time to react, he had slapped her. The left side of her face was burning and her head snapped back. Her leg had stretched to stop her from rolling backwards and her foot kicked the rice bowl off the tray. The bowl tumbled to the ground with rice spiraling out of it.

The man leaned forward with his fists pushed into the bed. His face was close to hers and she realized that he was afraid. This was sheer panic in his eyes.

"What. Did. He. Say?"

"We didn't really meet him. He just came up to us. He said that he is a 'Guardian of Time'... I have no idea what that means – is that some religious sect here? And then he said that he needed something from us. Frankly, I thought he was begging for money. And then he started to expose himself and Dean and I were about to walk away when you killed him."

She started to cry. She wanted to cry to distract the man even further, but right then she felt like crying anyway. What a mess. She was stuck in the middle of China with the guy who had just won the price for the Year's Stupidest Gangster. She now remembered the murder she had witnessed just the day before. She felt horrible and the crying was pretty good therapy.

THE MAN JUMPED back and screamed something in Chinese. Spittle fell on her arms. He was bright red in his face and he was still screaming at nobody specifically when he turned away from her and left the room. His bodyguard and the Hey-Lovely-guy followed and slapped the door shut.

Steps walked away and then came back hurriedly. The key turned in the lock.

34

"SCISSORS."

"Rock."

Mike touched Dean's outstretched fingers and pulled his fist back. "Well, I guess I'm doing the dirty half of the job today." He turned and smiled at Jia who was standing next to them on the roof of the Suzhou Hotel.

The red light of the sunset had turned Jia into a golden goddess, with a light wind lazily playing with her straight, black hair. She shaded her face with her left hand and tried to smile back, but she was too nervous and only managed a slightly upturned grin. "Please be careful down there."

"Always." Mike leaned forward and gave her a quick kiss, somehow now self-conscious in the presence of Dean. While they had all agreed that Karen must be alive, the thought of her getting murdered by Yau's men was never far away.

Mike and Dean checked each others climbing gear and Mike swung himself onto the edge of the chimney. His DynaRola-branded helmet flared up red in the last rays of the sun. He gave them both a smile and a thumbs up and descended into the hotel.

THEY HAD BEEN studying Dean's photos from his first descent into the hidden attic above room 517 and Mike knew what to look out for. He was whistling a silent tune, like he always did when working in climbing gear, subconsciously regulating his breathing to the rhythm of the climb. He got to the door in less than two minutes and wasn't even breathing hard. He pushed with one foot and completely opened the door. Dust billowed out again. He also noticed like Dean that the temperature in the attic was somehow odd. It felt like cold and warm air flooded over him out of the room at the same time.

Mike pulled himself into the attic and looked for the skeletal remains of Peter Koshitzky, knelt down and held his breath. He stared into the empty eye sockets of the dead man. After a moment he gave a small nod and stood up again. He toggled the walkie talkie. "I'm in. Peter..." He looked back at the skeleton. "...is where you left him."

"Everything else would have been a surprise. We are already setting up the rig. You should have the first basket down on your level in about ten minutes."

THEY HAD SPENT all morning wondering what to do, but finally decided that whatever else happened, they had to get ready to cut and run when they had Karen back. They needed money. Lot's of it. It was time for a withdrawal.

During the afternoon, Jia had visited her uncle with one of the gold bars and a business proposal. Mike and Dean had tracked down one of the few sporting goods stores in Shanghai and made some purchases that earned them strange looks and giggles from the clerks in the store.

Then the only thing left was to wait for sunset and for a call on the black cell phone. The call never came.

Mike had brought his power tool, with a circular saw blade attached. There was not going to be any monkeying around with a hand saw like last time. He started setting up lights next to the entrance and in the corners of his side of the room until the attic was comfortably bright.

He took the rest of the gold bars out of the box that Dean had opened and then closed the box and moved it to the very end of the room. He then started cutting through the lock of the next box, emptied it and again moved it to the end of the room, creating there a new stack of empty boxes.

HE DID A quick count of boxes that seemed to contain gold. There were thirtyseven stacks of five each. A hundred and eightyfive boxes! They had planned on stealing about twenty boxes worth of Yau's gold and it would be ridiculously easy to do that and hide the fact from whoever would come next and check the contents of the attic.

He estimated that it would take him about ten minutes per box. He hit the walkie talkie. "Dean."

"Yes?"

"How is it going?"

"The first basket should be in front of the door. Any ghosts yet?"

"No, just me and old Peter. Oh... and about fifty million dollars worth of gold."

"Holy shit. That's more than I would have thought even after seeing the boxes with my own eyes. So the plan will work?"

"Yep. Expect a delivery about every five minutes or so. We won't be able to put more than ten bars into one basket. Maybe even less than that."

Mike moved over to the chimney and pulled the first hanging basket into the attic. It was a heavy-duty grocery basket that would usually have been attached to the luggage rack of a Chinese bicycle. They had bought half a dozen of the baskets and carabiners to hook them onto a rope. The rope for the basket was going through a pulley at the top that was hanging off a steel bar across the chimney opening. The steel bar was rated to a hundred pounds and came from a weight lifting set in the gym equipment section of the sports store.

Mike filled the basket with ten gold bars and slowly eased it back out into the chimney. "Basket is ready to go."

"Roger that."

The basket smoothly disappeared from view. Mike went back to sawing off locks from boxes. After several of the boxes had been emptied it had become a series of automatic movements and his mind started to drift. He found it very hard to concentrate and at one point almost severed a finger from his hand with the power tool.

"DEAN? YOU WERE right."

"Childhood memories?"

"Yes. Intense ones. Just now I had a crazy flashback to second grade. I was there. I can now give you a full list of the names of my classmates back then. This is crazy."

"It's those spheres in the other boxes behind you..."

Mike sighed deep, stretched his back and bent back down to the task at hand. "There are no ghosts. There are no ghosts. There are no ghosts..." He repeated under his breath.

He carried two of the boxes back into the corner and created an empty stack of four. Then he lifted a full box with shaking arms and topped the stack off. It looked like the group of full boxes next to it. Perfect. Mike nodded to himself and turned around.

He stopped.

DEAN HAD BEEN pulling baskets filled with gold out of the chimney for the last half hour. Even with the pulley it was still hard, repetitive work and he was sweating profusely. Next to him was a full basket on the ground and two empty ones.

Jia came across the roof behind the fake gables, pushing along a small handcart that was carrying another empty basket. She dropped off the basket and Dean lifted another full basket onto her cart. She slowly disappeared along the iron grid walkways, past the glass roof of the courtyard, around a spire on the other end of the building. Dean continued dropping and pulling baskets.

Around the corner on the other side of the building was a small dead-end alley filled with garbage cans and a pile of rotting vegetables at the very end. Across the street was the empty concrete backside of the Suzhou Hotel Annex, a new building that had just been completed and would open in a few months. For now, the alley between the two buildings was dark and unused.

ABOVE THE ALLEY Jia met her uncle, a short, squat, heavyset men of indeterminate age. He had jet black hair, bushy eyebrows over a pair of very fast moving eyes that never seemed to rest on anything for more then a second. He had a round face with full lips and a thin stubble beard. All he needed was a pipe and a Northwester hat to look like a picture-book whaling captain. He was often underestimated because of his looks and regularly used this to his advantage in his business.

They exchanged a few words in Chinese, laughed, and he lifted the basket off Jia's cart, hooked it onto another rope and lowered it over the side of the building. The gold glinted in the light of a sole street lamp at the entrance of the alley. He had to push hard against the pull of the rope to keep his footing on the walkway. A minute later the weight of the basket had gradually disappeared and he pulled the empty basket back up.

His son, Jia's cousin, was sitting in the open back of a refrigerator-green truck in the shadows of the alley, chain-smoking unfiltered cigarettes and unloading baskets of gold bars every few minutes.

THE WALKIE TALKIE beeped. "Dean!"

"Yes." Dean used his arm to wipe sweat off his forehead.

"I... I am not exactly alone anymore." Mike voice was hushed, almost a whisper.

Dean had goosebumps marching across his back like armies during maneuvers. "The shadows?"

"Oh, there is not many shadows down here. I've lit up the place pretty good. But every now and then when I turn around, it looks like... shapes just disappear in thin air. Apparitions? Is that the word?" A long pause. Dean saw Jia coming back with the cart. He gestured her to be quiet. She slowed down and tiptoed closer.

"The last one I just saw was an orange shape, like it was wearing a robe!" Dean could hear Mike breathing heavily.

"What is happening?" Dean felt like shouting. He wanted to be down there. He wanted to run away. His heart was racing.

Jia stood still next to the walkie talkie, her eyes wide open and the mouth forming a big 'O', her arms wrapped around herself.

"It disappeared again. This is weird, it looked so solid, as if I could touch it... and then it just dissolves into thin air." Mike did sound shaken, but calm. "It always seems to show up near one of the smaller boxes over on the other side and then just disappears!"

"Are you OK?" Jia's voice was almost like a wail.

"Yes, honey. I'm completely OK. I almost peed my pants, and my world view has just quit on me, but I'm fine. Dean?"

"Yes."

"That box is next. I just looked at it, it is made from different wood than the others. This... thing wanted me to do something. And I think I'm supposed to not forget to take that box."

"You sure about that?"

"Well, if he... it doesn't like it, it can always come back and hit me with a clue stick."

Dean had to laugh at that. Mike was completely unflappable.

THE BOX ARRIVED next. It was another one of the smaller cube-shaped boxes that contained the spheres, but it was made from dark wood. Dean noticed something and used his flashlight to take a closer look. The box had markings on the outside. He had not seen that with any of the other boxes. It was the same strange writing system that they had seen engraved on the spheres. He stowed the box carefully in his backpack.

After that more gold arrived. It was after 11pm when Mike stopped clearing out boxes. He rearranged the contents of the room so that the five stacks that contained the empty boxes were hidden behind several rows of boxes still full of gold. He had dusted off all the boxes so that none of them looked any more or less untouched. Only a dedicated audit would reveal what had happened.

MIKE HAD SEVERAL more strange episodes of flashbacks, all of them taking him back to earliest childhood memories. It seemed as if the spheres somehow were stirring up long forgotten thoughts and feelings in his brain, and he had to fight hard to concentrate on the here and now.

He looked around the room one more time, and then one after another switched off the lights. Only his helmet light pierced the darkness, and dust was dancing in the lonely beam, creating new shapes over and over, unseen for all time.

Mike climbed into the chimney and pulled the small door shut. He took a deep breath and started climbing.

35

IT HAD BEEN a long day. Karen had not spoken to anyone since the man in the gray suit had tried to interrogate her. She had heard the sound of a car engine a few times and once several people had been walking past her room, but otherwise there was nothing to do. All she had was the TV with its soap operas and news shows in Chinese.

She had opened the curtains and the window and had let some air into the room. There was a row of vertical steel bars in front of the window, not as thick as in a prison - maybe about the width of a pencil each, but still strong enough to hold her in. There was not much of a view, the room was facing north towards a thicket of bamboo mixed in with dense underbrush. The sound of the wind in the trees was soothing and lulled her into a half-sleep for most of the afternoon.

At eight o'clock the Hey-Lovely-guy was back, pushing another plate of fried rice and vegetables into the room. He said no word and was not even looking at her. This time he didn't forget to lock the door.

SHE WAS ABOUT to fall asleep when suddenly the crickets in front of her window stopped their summer-night concert. She heard a soft footstep in the grass outside and looked up from the bed.

There was an orange silhouette in front of her room. Her stomach bunched together and panic rose. It was the monk in the orange robe! She gasped and pushed herself away from the window.

The monk came to the window in one quick step, pulled the top of the robe back to reveal his face and put a finger on his lips.

Karen collapsed on the bed again and breathed heavily. It was a different man. Of course it was. Panic was slowly replaced by hope. She looked at his face, raising one eyebrow in an unspoken question.

The man had an open and honest face with dark-tanned skin. He was still young, maybe nineteen or twenty years old with bright, clear eyes and a winning smile with a full set of white teeth reflecting the light from her room.

HE WENT TO the center of the window and grabbed two of the steel bars. The orange robe fell back and revealed two arms bulging with muscles. His smile was replaced by a look of concentration with the tip of his tongue sticking out between his lips.

Karen could not believe what she saw, but the steel bars started to bend, slowly, ever so slowly. They originally were about three inches apart, but where the man's hands grabbed them, this distance had already doubled. She could hear the cracking of the mortar as it slowly gave way and the two steel bars were only hanging on at the top of the window frame. Now the man started bending the next two bars until they gave and then another set. The whole time she couldn't hear anything from him, not even a breath.

The hole was now easily big enough for her. The man stepped back and gestured to her. She looked around, but there was nothing to bring along. She put on her sneakers, went to the door, switched off the light and then she climbed onto the bed and through the steel bars.

It occurred to her that she must be developing quite a name in the Triad grapevine. She had twice beaten up their gunmen and now she seemingly all by herself had escaped from a hostage prison. She smiled at that thought, jumped down from the window frame and hugged the man, monk or not.

THERE WAS A small sliver of the moon visible in the sky and it gave a little bit of light. Behind them was the building she had just escaped from and otherwise the only thing visible was the huge bamboo grove in front of them. A light wind played in the tall bamboo stalks and they swayed in a slow motion, low creaks emitting from where they rubbed against each other.

The man took her hand in his and slowly, without any hurry, walked in between the tall bamboo. They made a little noise, but it was far less than Karen had been afraid of.

His hand felt unnaturally warm around hers.

36

DEAN, MIKE AND Jia stood behind the truck in the dead-end alley. They reverently looked at the small pile of yellow metal bars that were currently being covered with a camouflage-patterned tarp by Jia's cousin. He jumped from the back of the truck and closed the cargo door. He turned around and smiled at Dean.

Jia made introductions. "Dean, this is Zhou. He's my cousin and if he doesn't drop out of university altogether – and that's an even bet if you ask me, then he'll one day take over my uncle's business."

Zhou had now a wide smile on his face. He held out a hand. "Nice to meet." His English was limited, but his face spoke all by itself. He had one of those faces that can in mere seconds transition through a whole range of emotions. Dean earmarked him as a model for a future photo shoot.

They shook hands. "Nice to meet you. And thank you for helping us."

"Your friend will... is... OK?"

"Yes, I hope so. I'm sure we will find her soon. Thank you." Dean was glad that he was surrounded by so many people that genuinely cared for Karen and him. Without them he would not know what to do.

Dean had been expecting a phone call from Yau's gang sometime today and he was very worried about their silence. He had already checked a hundred times if the little LED was still blinking.

THEY ALL PILED into the cab of the truck, with Dean and Mike sharing the emergency seats behind the first row with the driver and passenger seats. Zhou was driving. The truck came to life with a low rumble, Diesel fumes were wafting through the cabin. The transmission had seen better days and the truck jerked out of the alley as if it was complaining about the half ton of gold that was now on its cargo bed.

They drove through Shanghai's night, through empty side streets and dark alleyways. Zhou was trying to avoid the main arteries through the city with their continuous police presence, but this meant that they had to take quite a detour through some of the less developed areas of the metropolis.

There were areas where houses had fallen in disrepair, where whole city blocks had been razed to the ground for another futuristic building project. It was by now after midnight, but gangs of migrant workers were still hard at work demolishing more buildings with nothing but sledge hammers, their naked upper bodies glistening with sweat.

The truck passed factories, lit up bright, their smokestacks topped with clouds of billowing smoke. Even now in the early morning hours of a new day, tens of thousands of people were working everywhere. Dean felt a great energy in this city - it was a place with a purpose, hard at work.

DEAN HAD BEEN dreamily staring out the window when the truck stopped. They had reached a warehouse in the outskirts of Shanghai, next to a canal that was lined with small freighters. When they left the cab of the truck, he could smell the stink of the oily water in the canal. There was a continuous splash as small waves got caught between the boats and the walls of the canal.

Jia's uncle unlocked the gate of his warehouse and Zhou backed the truck against a large loading dock. They spent the next hour unloading the cold gold bars by hand, passing them from one person to the next, from hand to hand. They made a neat row of little stacks from the bars and the uncle counted them out loud.

They had 395 bars in the warehouse, plus the five that were already in his office. Mike looked at Dean with a grin on his face.

"We should do this more often."

37

KAREN WAS GLAD that she had been napping all afternoon. Her rescuer guided her through the bamboo thicket, up along a steep path through the hills, only lit by the moon. On over a ridge and down through a valley, across bridges and up again... she had lost track of time and space and was just walking along behind him, mile after mile.

He spoke a little English, but had up to now shown very little interest in talking to her, other than pure practicalities.

"I'm Karen. And what is your name?"

"Tseten. Careful – here are stairs!"

"Thanks. That doesn't sound like a Chinese name."

"From Tibet. It's name from Tibet. Now slippery."

That was the longest conversation they had in the first two hours of their hike.

THEY HAD JUST reached the ridge of another hill, when Karen saw an almost unearthly red glow emanating from the forest in front of them. Distinct, jagged black edges were visible against the night sky. She realized that they had reached the edge of an ancient temple complex, with the outlines of darkened buildings all around suddenly becoming visible to her.

The monk stopped and turned to her. "Please wait." He disappeared in the shadows.

Karen stood in the dark, with faint moonlight only touching the tops of the curved roofs around her and a soft red, flickering glow coming from one of the buildings ahead. She slowly turned all the way around, taking in the smells and sounds of the forest at night. There was also a faint smell of incense in the air.

She realized that some of the buildings were ruins and what had only been a suspicion became a certainty. Yau had brought her to his ancestral home. The building she had escaped from must have been his father's house in... what had been the name of the province?

Hubei? She tried to remember. No... Hunan!

Karen turned around in another slow circle. So this was the temple of the Guardians of Time!

SHE CHECKED HER watch in the dim moonlight. It was just after eleven o'clock, so they had been hiking for almost two hours. It felt good to stand still, but sitting down would be even nicer. Her eyes had adjusted to the shadows and she saw stairs leading up to a burnt out building on her left. She sat down on the stairs and stretched her legs. Broken roof tiles crunched under her feet. Complex shadows and thin, silvery strips of moonlight criss-crossed the temple ruin. Several trees had grown large in the hall and their crowns now combined into a new, natural roof for the building.

She could hear the voices of a small group of men before she saw their dark shapes, backlit by the glow from the building behind them. Karen recognized the shorter shape on the right as Tseten, her rescuer from Yau's prison. Two robed men stood with him as they searched the courtyard for her. Tseten pointed to the burned ruin and said something. They came over with unhurried steps and stood before her. They gave her a slight bow. Karen was too tired to stand up and just nodded back.

"WE ARE SORRY that we can not offer you any hospitality, but this temple..." The man in the center waved an arm around. "This temple is not a safe place to stay, Miss Chadbourne. You have made a dangerous enemy in Martin Yau, and he will try everything to capture you again."

Karen was incredulous. "You know my name?"

"One of our associates was in Shanghai when you and your friends discovered the..." He broke off and said something in Chinese.

Karen interrupted "Spheres?"

"Yes. Spheres. He was able to find you and he reported to us. Did he... contact you?"

Karen shuddered. The memories of Yu Yuan Garden were still too fresh. "He was murdered! Yau's men shot him when he tried to talk us. I am sorry."

The man nodded. He spoke in Chinese to the quiet men to his right. Tseten on his left had turned around and was scanning the forest behind them.

Karen leaned back on her elbows. The monks had made no moves to accommodate her and she had the feeling this would be a long night.

The man turned back to her. "You and Tseten will have to continue soon. You have a long way in front of you. Are you comfortable to walk further? It may take all night."

Karen had never walked all night. She had a hard time thinking of what kind of distance they were talking about. But it couldn't be helped. She had only one chance to get away from Yau, and if it meant walking, so be it. She got up. "I'm OK. Thank you for rescuing me."

"Oh. You are welcome. But you have to realize, your rescue is only a small battle in a bigger war. We help you to escape, but only because we will gain more by keeping you out of the reach of Yau." He turned away and they all started walking towards the dark forest. "We have been waiting for sixty years, both us and Mr. Yau. And now the day is here."

The two tall, hooded men stopped. Karen and Tseten turned back to them.

"You and your friends have unleashed a fight to the death between us and Mr. Yau's organization. When you get back to Shanghai, I would like you to warn your friends. Stay away from the spheres!" He raised his arm. "Good Bye, Miss Chadbourne."

She nodded. "Good Bye. And thank you." She turned around and followed Tseten into the cool, dark bamboo forest.

THEY TOOK A different path down the hill, and after about half an hour they entered a large plain of rice paddies. Tseten guided her along narrow, elevated paths between the rice fields and she had to concentrate hard not to slip off and step into the water that flooded the fields. They had to walk behind each other and there was no chance for Karen to ask questions.

The silence gave her a lot of time to think, but she had a hard time to concentrate on her predicament. It took her several hours to figure out that she had actually no direct way to talk to Mike, Jia and Dean. Even if she made it to a phone and managed to call somebody in Shanghai, who would she call? The best bet was to leave a message in the Suzhou Hotel.

They did meet people on some of the paths, farmers coming home late from the fields or migrant workers on their way from one village to the next. They acknowledged each other with a grunt or a short greeting, with the monk keeping up their side of the encounter. Since Karen had slightly American Indian features and dark hair, none of the people who saw her in the weak moonlight tagged her as a foreigner.

IT WAS AROUND one o'clock in the morning when they stopped for a rest near a small village. One of the houses had a lone light bulb hanging in front of a window. It was the local equivalent of a 24-hour convenience store catering to the village-to-village travelers on this dirt path. Tseten woke the old woman behind the window with a loud greeting and bought some fruits and two bottles of water. They sat at the side of the path in the dark and ate apples.

The moon had set and only the stars were lighting up this landscape of rice paddies and rounded hills overgrown with bamboo. Small villages were visible only because of one or two lights out in the open, usually close to the communal outhouses.

It was the most rural place that Karen had ever visited and the infrastructure seemed to date back to the 18th century, but up to now all the people they had met on the road seemed to be content, with a friendly smile on their faces.

"Where are we going?"

"There is a river. There is..." The monk was searching for the words. "Harbor." She could see his white smile even by the light of the stars. "There is ship. To Shanghai."

"We are taking a boat? All the way to Shanghai? I came here by plane!" She felt slightly stupid when she said that.

He was waving his hands back and forward. "No... airport. Private."

"Oh. I see." So common folk used the ships. There would be no more executive transport for her.

THEY ARRIVED IN a small town with the first brightening of the sky just before dawn. Karen was exhausted, but the excitement of the escape had pumped so much adrenaline through her body that she wouldn't be able to sleep until she was safely on the boat.

They walked through darkened streets under a violently pink sky, surrounded by the sounds of a town waking up for another day of work. She had already noticed in Shanghai that street life in China starts early with the sunrise. She was astonished to already see a group of old ladies - none of them under eighty - doing morning exercises at half past five in the morning, with a little boom box providing Olivia Newton-John's "Physical" as background music.

Tseten brought her down to the river front, where among decrepit warehouses was a dock for the local ferry. There was already a ship preparing to leave, with people carrying suitcases, car parts and livestock in cages onto the ship. The dock area was busy with a thousand things happening at the same time.

The monk walked through the chaos with his orange robe parting the crowd like a bow wave. The appearance of a foreign woman behind him stopped all conversation on the dock. The people in this town obviously were not used to seeing foreign faces among them.

Tseten bought two tickets from an old woman with a portable desk at the side of the pier and they made it onto the boat with only minutes to spare. By six o'clock sharp the ropes were hauled in and the boat slowly turned into the river and headed downstream.

THE MONK TOUCHED her shoulder and pointed to the pier behind them. "Look!"

Karen turned from the rather interesting impromptu village opera being played out on deck. She gasped. There on the pier stood a camouflaged open jeep with wide dirt marks up along the sides. In it stood her interrogator from the day before, screaming and gesticulating at the top of his lungs. In the driver's seat was the Hey-Lovely-guy, his forehead leaning against the wheel in exhaustion.

Karen made sure that they recognized her by stepping to the railing of the deck. The man stopped screaming and looked directly at her across a hundred yards of open water, the distance becoming wider with every second.

Karen slowly lifted the right hand and stretched her middle finger into the air.

38

HE WAS RUNNING away from a ghost. He could not see the ghost, because every time he turned around it disappeared into the shadows. But he knew it was there and he kept on running. The shadows behind him got closer and closer, no matter how fast he ran. The ground changed, it was suddenly wooden boards. He looked up. He was in the attic in the Suzhou Hotel. The skeleton was gone, but the dead monk was sitting in its place. Suddenly the monk's eyes opened, he got up and stood before Dean. The monk started to speak, but Dean only heard a cell phone ring. The monk's mouth opened again. The cell phone rang again. The cell phone... the cell phone!

DEAN WOKE UP with a start. He was sitting bolt upright in bed in his suite in the Suzhou Hotel. He was covered in sweat. He jumped up, got entangled in the sheets and fell out of bed trying to reach the ringing cell phone on the table.

He finally managed to reach the phone and grabbed it, on his knees in front of the table. He flipped it open. "Hello!"

"Mr. Lashure? Good morning."

"What? Yes. This is Lashure." He was rubbing the sleep out of his eyes with one hand and squeezed the tiny phone against his ear with the other. He fell back and sat on the carpet with his shoulder against the foot of the bed. It was not even dawn yet and the city was shrouded in darkness.

"We have some business to discuss." The voice was very refined and smooth with a distinct British accent.

"Where is Karen?" He looked at the glowing red numbers of the alarm clock on the night stand – it was only five – he had slept for less than three hours.

"Oh... we have her in a safe place." Dean could hear something like a jet engine in the background. Was this man at the airport? He realized that he had to wake Mike right now to track the call. He jumped up and opened the connecting door to the other suite.

"I would like to talk to her!" He entered the other suite. Jia and Mike were both sleeping deeply. Mike grabbed a balled up pair of socks from a chair and threw them straight at Mike's head. Mike woke with a start. "Hmm... what!" Dean had just enough time to cover the microphone.

"I am right now in transit, but I assure you she is OK. And if you want to keep it that way, I have to insist that you listen to me closely." That man was getting on Dean's nerves with his smooth we-are-old-chaps way of talking.

MIKE LOOKED UP and saw him talk on the black cell phone. He ran naked over to the desk and with a touch to the mouse woke the laptop from its sleep. He started typing furiously.

"We want the photographs you have."

Dean stared at an empty spot on the wall. The meaning of this request hit him like a fist in the stomach. They had no idea! Yau's gang had no idea where they were or that they already had found the gold. This was too good to be true.

"Uhm... OK. I think I have no other choice."

"No, you don't. Should we not be able to get the photos from you, you will never see Chadbourne again. Do you understand?"

"But I want an exchange. I will only give you the pictures if you bring Karen to the meeting. If I don't see her, no pictures." He had to lean against the door frame. He felt dizzy. He was gambling with Karen's life.

"Very well. I will arrange for her to be brought to Shanghai tonight. We will meet in Pudong. Close to the new airport is a construction site for the Millennium Star Hotel. It's just off the highway, almost finished, with a big golden star on the roof. We will meet you in front of the entrance of the building tonight at eleven sharp. If you don't bring the photos, we will kill her. If we see police, we will kill her. If you are not alone, we will kill her. Do you understand?"

Mike looked up from the laptop. He lifted his right hand, thumb outstretched.

"Yes. Tonight at eleven o'clock. At the Millennium Star construction site. I will be there, alone."

"Good." The line went dead.

"WHAT AN ASSHOLE!" Dean had to restrain himself from dropping the phone in disgust.

Mike was triumphant. "I got him! He has been calling from Jinshi in northern Hunan province." He turned to Dean. "That's way out in the sticks, about an hours worth of flight time from here."

"I heard a jet engine in the background... is there an airport in that place?"

Mike had become aware that he had been sitting at the desk naked and he casually wrapped a towel around his hips. "Man, I have no idea. But even if there is one, there won't be many flights. I guess they are using a private plane, or they've cut a deal with the military. The Chinese military operates like a private company and it is possible to pay them for services. Illegal, but not unheard of."

Mike sat down on the bed and gave Jia a quick kiss. She had been sitting up in bed during the discussion and was listening closely.

Dean was sill leaning against the door frame. "This guy said that they'd bring Karen along. We are going to meet at the Millennium Star Hotel construction site at eleven tonight."

"That's out near the new airport. I know that place – in fact, I've been to the roof of that building already." Mike had become thoughtful and he was scratching his unshaven chin. "I may be able..." He turned back to his computer. "Since I have now the network ID of his phone, I will be able to track his location automatically every time he calls somebody over our network. I'll set it up so that we get a report from this computer for each new location. This way we know when they arrive in town."

"Really?" Dean was impressed. "It's scary that you can do this!"

"Yeah... it wouldn't be possible in the States since the cell networks are pretty old and well locked down. But since we are still building this network here in China, a lot of the security measures are not in place. Most of the contractors with us here in the city pretty much have absolute power over the network, since we are changing stuff all the time. You don't want to hang off a rope at the tip of a skyscraper and discover that you have to call your boss' boss' boss to get something switched off."

39

KAREN AND TSETEN were sitting on the open upper deck in the sun, with their back against the warm, white steel wall of the first class sitting room. The bridge of the boat was another ten feet above them. The ship had two main decks around a core that contained on the lower deck a small kitchen that dispensed cheap food in styrofoam containers. Behind the kitchen were the unspeakably dirty bathrooms.

On the upper deck the core held a small first class lobby with upholstered seats around little daintily decorated side tables. A few older passengers sat in there, playing mahjong and chain smoking all day, while the rest of the passengers sat under the open sky on the upper deck. The lower deck was mostly crammed full with whatever luggage and cargo the passengers had brought on board. There was a lot of produce in large baskets, large machine parts and a surprising array of live animals in cages of all shapes and sizes.

TSETEN HAD TOLD her that this trip would take about six hours to a larger town on the Yangtze river and then they would have to take another boat overnight to Shanghai. She had just stared at him, unbelieving of what she had heard. Another one and a half days on a boat?

"Tseten, I will have to buy a few things in the next town. Can you borrow me some money?"

He looked at her without comprehending.

Karen simplified her question. "Give me some money!" She pointed at her dirty shirt and she made the motion of brushing her teeth.

His face lit up and he smiled his toothy smile at her. "Yes!" He reached into his robe and pulled a small bundle of Chinese bills out of some sort of leather pouch that he had hanging around his neck. He rolled off about two dozen of the bills and gave them to her. "On next boat – you, me – sleeping together."

Her eyebrows rose in surprise and she stared at him. But he was still just cheerfully smiling at her. She thought this was worth clarifying.

"We sleep in the same cabin? Two beds?" She held up two fingers.

Tseten bunched his brows together in thought, but finally it dawned on him what she thought he had said. "Oh – yes, yes, yes!" His hands made a little dance of two separate flat objects that seemed to move away from each other. "Two beds! Not one bed! One... cabin?" He nodded and laughed, his ears red with embarrassment.

She had now 250 Yuan Renminbi, or about thirty dollars to work with. She knew that this was almost a month's income in the villages she had been walking through last night.

It was too bad Tseten had such a hard time with English, since she had so many questions for him and it seemed that they would have a lot of time to talk before they would make it back to Shanghai.

How had he known that she would be at Yau's building in those hills? Why were they interfering with Yau's plans? Who were the Guardians of Time? Where did those spheres come from and what did they actually do?

She sighed, closed her eyes and leaned back to enjoy the sun.

SEVERAL HOURS LATER Karen was standing at the bow of the boat on the lower deck, leaning against a large shipping crate that, at least from the signs on it, seemed to contain a new motorcycle. With her left hand she was holding a styrofoam container with about thirty cents worth of spicy fried rice with tofu and cabbage and with the chopsticks in her right she was enthusiastically shoveling the food into her mouth. It was delicious and the hike through the hills last night had left her very hungry.

It was by now a gloriously hot and sunny day and the wind from the moving boat was cooling her down just enough. If she could just tell her friends in Shanghai that she was OK, then she could actually relax and enjoy this trip. But since that would probably not be possible at all, she would be sitting on coals all the way to Shanghai.

The river was busy with small watercraft of all kinds. It wasn't a particularly big river, maybe 150 feet across, and so all the different boats spent a lot of their energy on avoiding collisions. A symphony of horns, bells, whistles and shouts hung over the water as the captains of the vessels signaled each other.

Karen was utterly fascinated by all of this activity and somehow was already looking forward to the trip down the Yangtze river. She noticed that the banks of the river had changed over the last half hour. It seemed that they were getting close to a larger town and suddenly factories and small warehouses made out of rusty corrugated sheet metal were replacing the rice paddies.

This had to be their destination on this river. She went back to the upper deck to find Tseten.

40

MIKE CAME INTO Dean's suite and walked up to where Dean was sitting at the desk facing the window. He was looking at the busy river scene in front of the hotel with unseeing eyes, deep in thought.

"The man you've been talking to arrived in Shanghai at six this morning, got a call from the Jinshi area and get this, immediately went back to Jinshi! By eight he was back in Hunan and then he went crazy with his phone. He's been calling local numbers in Jinshi five times in half an hour, to Hong Kong three times and then he made several calls to Shanghai, Wuhan and Huangshi. All that before nine thirty. Then he has been quiet for about two hours and now he's popped up again here in Shanghai and since then he has spent almost an hour on the phone with Hong Kong. Busy man."

Dean had been looking at the photos he had printed from the film in Mr. Chadbourne's camera. He sighed. "When we give these pictures to Yau's men, they will know where to look for the gold. They'll be here in the hotel by midnight tonight, ripping the furniture out of room 517."

Mike was a little disappointed that his report had not even been acknowledged by Dean. He looked at Dean closer. He was unshaven, had dark rings under his eyes, and his T-Shirt was stained with sweat.

"Man, you don't look good. I'd suggest you take a bit of a rest this afternoon. We'll need you at a hundred percent tonight."

Dean's hands were shaking as he pushed them back through his hair. He sighed. "I know. It's just... I can't stop thinking about what Karen is going through right now. For all we know she is locked up in some basement in Hunan province. Why out there anyway? Couldn't they find a closer spot to hide her?"

"I've spent some time thinking about that. Remember our meeting with Helen Turner? She said that Martin Yau's father was a warlord in Hunan province and that when he died, Martin inherited everything. That's also where the temple of the Guardians of Time was, before it was destroyed."

"Oh – so you think that Yau still owns property out there? Shouldn't he have lost it when the communists took over?"

"Nothing in China is ever that absolute and Hunan is far from Beijing. Even if he lost it officially, he had so much money that he probably just bought the whole thing back in the Eighties when the Chinese government started to loosen up a bit on land ownership."

"Maybe we can talk to Helen and see if we can find where in Hunan his property was."

"I bet you dollars to donuts that it is near Jinshi." Mike saw the flicker in Dean's eyes. "And no, we are not going to invest our five million dollars in gold into half-assed rescue schemes for Karen. They are bringing her here tonight, remember?"

DEAN LOOKED AWAY, out the window at the river. "I'm sorry... I can't think straight right now. Do you think this would maybe be the right time to call the cops?"

Mike shrugged. "Not really. The police here in town is very effective in organizing traffic detours. But especially with crimes involving foreigners, they have quite a heavy hand. And they'll first of all assume that whoever they got is at least partially guilty. There's a chance they'll just lock us up for a day or two so they can sort out our stories. And how do you want to explain the stuff in the attic? Once they find the gold and the skeleton, Karen will be way down on their list of priorities."

Mike was padding his pockets. "Anyway, I've been doing some organizing for tonight. Here." He gave Dean another DynaRola cell phone. "When you are about to meet Yau's men tonight, speed-dial the first number in the address book. This way I will be able to listen in to what's going on. I will be at Pudong airport in one of the parking lots with – I hope – some reinforcements. Jia went over to her uncle's office and the two of them are going to hire a few bodyguards for tonight."

DEAN THREW THE cell phone from hand to hand. "There is another thing..." He looked Mike in the eyes. "About Helen Turner."

"What about her?"

"Do you think she could have told Yau's gang about our conversation? I've been thinking about this all morning, but it doesn't really make sense one way or another."

Mike sat down on the edge of the bed. He was staring past Dean out the window, his eyebrows pulled together in concentration. "Oh... I see. The sphere."

Dean nodded. "The sphere. If Helen would have told Yau about the sphere, his goons would not be asking for the pictures. They think we haven't found the spheres yet. Helen knows we have. Why would she tell him where we are but not what we have shown her? And if she didn't tell Yau about us, how on earth did those people find us in the Yu Yuan Garden? It doesn't make sense!"

Mike pulled up an eyebrow. "Somebody else saw us there and knew our names."

"Of course!" Dean hit the desk with his open hand. "The assistant! She never saw the sphere!"

41

THEIR BOAT MANEUVERED itself into position behind a much larger vessel on a floating pier along the river. As their boat bumped into the wooden pilings and ropes were thrown across to a crew of men on the pier, Tseten pointed at the city in front of them.

"This is Huangshi. And this -" He pointed at the huge ferry in front of their boat. "- is ship to Shanghai. We leave at... one thirty." He was looking at her to see if she understood.

Karen checked her watch. It was now half past twelve, so she had almost an hour to supply herself for the next thirty hours of traveling down the river.

They were with the first group of passengers to come of the boat, since they had no luggage to slow them down. Behind them several dozen farmers were sorting out a multitude of livestock crises on the lower deck of the boat.

Tseten took her arm. He pointed at the gangway to the Yangtze ferry. "I have to wait in line for ticket. We meet there. One fifteen. OK?"

So much for the phone call – without him she had no chance to even find a phone. But they needed the tickets, so there was nothing she could do. "OK. I will be here at one fifteen."

Tseten nodded, let go of her arm and walked to a long line for tickets over at the end of the pier. Karen looked after him, a lone orange-robed figure slowly moving through the hustle and bustle of the river port.

She realized that she was now completely alone in the middle of China, with 250 Yuan in her pocket and no papers. She couldn't speak the language and had no idea where in China she actually was other than the name of the city. Huangshi.

It didn't mean anything to her, but it was obviously a big city. From what she had seen along the riverbanks, it looked bigger than San Francisco and seemed to have more large industry than the area around Chicago.

ACROSS THE STREET from the riverbank with its piers and ferry ramps was a long row of small department stores catering to the needs of the many travelers that arrived and left again on a steady stream of boats of all sizes. Karen chose one of the stores close to the pier that she had to go back to and just walked around for a few minutes, pushed along by a lively throng of shoppers. She was overwhelmed by the noise and the smells and all the things to see.

On the ground floor was mostly prepackaged food and some basic hygiene supplies, while upstairs she found a colorful collection of clothes, souvenirs, soft drinks, toys, ripoffs of western DVDs and CDs and a place to sign up for cell phone service.

She bought two T-shirts, a cap and some underwear in hues of pink that she wouldn't want to get caught dead in back in the States. She had to pay at a small booth in the corner and ended up just handing several random bills to the young girl at the cash register who then gave her almost all of it back, minus a small deduction for the cost of the goods. Karen figured that she had just spent a grand total of three dollars on clothes.

Downstairs she found some toothpaste, a toothbrush and a roll of toilet paper. One thing she had already learned on the first boat was that you strictly bring your own. She also picked up some chocolate, paid this time with more confidence and left the store in quite a triumphant mood.

KAREN STOOD IN front of the department store three stairs above the street level and scanned the area in front of the Shanghai boat to see if Tseten already had tickets. She finally found him still in the ticket line, close to the window. She had a few more minutes to look around.

When she turned away, her eyes caught two men standing next to the gangway that led to the Shanghai boat. She looked back. One of them was scanning the passengers as they walked past them, and the other man was sweeping up and down the port area with a small set of binoculars. He was currently looking straight at her.

Karen turned away rapidly and walked back into the store. She stopped and looked back. The man with the binoculars had tapped his partner's shoulder and he was already moving fast.

It was sixty feet from the gangway across the street to the store and it was a busy street. Karen twisted around into the store and pushed through dozens of shoppers that were blocking the narrow aisles. When she was in the store before she had seen a door in the back next to the stairs and now she made a beeline for it.

She was lucky and the door wasn't locked. She pulled it open, slipped through and shut it again. She was in the office of the store, with several desks pushed together in a narrow space, computers on the desks, calenders and various papers tacked to the walls. There was another door in the back and she hoped that it would lead out of the building. She belatedly realized that she had startled a woman working on one of the computers who was now watching her open-mouthed as she was running through the office.

The door was locked, but there was actually a key in the lock. Karen turned it and slipped through, blinded by sunlight.

"Yes! Whoa!"

She slipped and almost fell off the loading dock with its sleek metal surface. To her left was another door into the storage room of the store, and beyond were similar doors to the offices and storage spaces of all the other stores that opened to the street along the harbor.

KAREN STOPPED FOR a moment to breathe and work on a plan. She had to get back to the ship. By now, Tseten should have bought the tickets and he would be waiting at the gangway. Yau's men were looking for her in the store. She pulled one of the t-shirts out of the shopping bag. It was a bright red shirt with "Beijing 2008" imprinted across the front. She pulled it over the long-sleeved, white shirt she had been wearing for the last few days. She also put on the red cap she had bought. It wasn't great, but it was as good as it would get.

She walked to her left down along the loading dock and casually jumped over a small gap to the next loading dock. A man was unloading boxes from a truck and she walked past with a quick nod. He had not even realized that she was a foreigner.

Another jump across to the next loading dock. She opened the next door that she passed and walked in without a look back. It was a dark storage room. The little light that came into the room came from the cracks in the door behind her and the door in front of her.

She had no time to wait for her eyes to adjust, so she just kept on walking towards the door to the store. She hit her shin on a box and the pain made her eyes water. She stumbled and fell to her knees. *Never mind – keep on walking.*

She pushed the door open and stood behind the counter of a bakery. It smelled beautifully of fresh bread. Two women in white uniforms stood behind the counter with her and stared in surprise. One of them started shaking across her whole body and then she cracked up laughing. The other one was cracking up, too. Across the counter the customers joined in laughter.

Karen realized that the floor in the storage room had been covered with flour and by patting herself down after her near-fall she had covered herself in white hand-prints from her face down all across her bright red t-shirt. She had to join in the laughter and she bowed to apologize to the two shop employees. She nonchalantly opened a gate in the counter and walked through the cheerful crowd out into the street.

A quick look left and right, she couldn't see the two men. Maybe they were still in the first store. She walked across the street in a fast trot dodging several bicyclists, going straight for the gangway. She now spotted Tseten's orange robe, he was standing exactly where the two men had been waiting for her only a few minutes ago.

She heard a shout from the left. She glanced over her shoulder quickly. There was the guy who had spotted her originally. He was standing in the door of the first store pointing at her and shouting something into the store to his buddy.

SHE STARTED TO run.

She had to jump over cages with chickens and piles of suitcases. She pushed people aside and almost fell when she tried to avoid a collision with a small girl.

She ran.

"Tseten! Help!"

He had spotted her and saw her pointing to her left. He turned his attention to the two men that were running across the street, barely avoiding a large truck and several bicycles.

Karen made it to the gangway first. She passed Tseten who pressed a ticket in her hand. She crammed the ticket in her jeans and turned around going into a fighting stance as her teacher had spent so many hours to perfect on her.

Tseten below her stood in the middle of the narrow gangway, effectively blocking it. He stood there with his legs and arms wide. His hands were open and relaxed. It was very different from what Karen would have expected after a lifetime of exposure to Kung-Fu movies.

THE TWO MEN came running up to the dock. One of them came screaming up to Tseten, while the other had slowed down, reaching for something under his jacket. Hundreds of people on the dockside had either seen them running past or had now heard the screams.

Everybody turned towards them. For Karen, high up on the gangway, it looked like sunflowers turning into the sun, with more and more faces in the shadows of the buildings being lit up by the sun-drenched ship with its white paint. A wave of bright faces expanding away from them in all directions.

Tseten jumped.

Time splintered like a fallen mirror.

Some things slowed down. Others sped up. Tseten's left foot had hit the man in front square in the face. She saw ripples running across his face as the shock wave ran its course. Tseten's right foot had lightly touched the guardrail of the gangway and catapulted him in a cartwheel across the man, their two heads almost touching each other.

Karen sucked in air. She was in shock. She could not move, her muscles frozen, like in a dream. She saw people's faces in the crowd turn away. They did not see this like she did!

Tseten had landed in front of the second man who now held a gun in his right hand. He had it just out of his jacket when

Tseten came close to him. To Karen it looked like the monk was embracing the man with his hands diving under the man's jacket. They froze. Tseten moved away again.

Time healed.

THERE SHE WAS, in a picture book perfect fighting stance. Some people in the crowd still stared at her, but most had started to turn away and were laughing at themselves. Nothing to see here. Closer by, people were kneeling down to help the two men who had fallen. Tseten was calmly walking up the gangway towards her. He picked up the shopping bag she had dropped.

"Go."

SHE TURNED AROUND as if in a trance and slowly stumbled up the gangway. Tseten was holding her from behind. His hand felt hot on her right arm. Behind her she heard new shouts from the crowd. She was sure the two men were dead.

There was a ship's officer at the top of the gangway and she pulled the ticket out of her jeans pocket. The man smiled at her like he had not just seen two men being killed in a fight. He gave her the ticket back and then he checked Tseten's ticket. He pointed them both to the front of the ship where they found the door to cabin 118.

TSETEN OPENED THE cabin door and stepped through. She followed him in and slapped the door shut. She leaned against the cold metal.

"OK. What the hell just happened? Did you kill these men?"

"Yes. They wanted to kill."

"How?" She sighed. "I mean... what was that? What happened there? Nobody else saw you do it. You flew through the air, killed two men with some amazing moves *and nobody else sees that?*"

He had climbed into the upper of the two bunks in the cabin and sat down on it crosslegged. "I am Guardian of Time."

A small fan under the ceiling was humming away, slowly turning left and right. It was woefully underpowered in this heat. A feeble puff of moving air hit her face.

"I know that. But what did you do out there? That was not just some martial art thing."

"Guardians of Time..." His teenage face went almost cross-eyed as he was desperately looking for words. "...touch time. We touch time like you touch this!" His hand patted the blanket on his bed.

Her mouth stood open. Was this possible? She remembered what it felt like when Dean had spun up the sphere in Mike's apartment. She remembered the... things... she had seen behind Dean in the video from the attic.

"Guardians of Time!" She whispered to herself.

<h1 style="text-align:center">42</h1>

MIKE SPEED-DIALED. "It's her direct line." He gave Dean a significant look while he waited for her to pick up.

"Helen, my love! How are you today?"

"Yeah... it's humid, isn't it? No, I'm certainly not climbing up a building if there's a chance of lightning, thank you very much." He laughed.

"Listen, we need your help again. Have you had a chance to look up any more information about Yau?"

Dean was pacing back and forward in front of the window.

"Near Jinshi? Really? That is indeed very helpful. Do you have the exact address?" He started to write. Dean came over and was amazed when he saw that Mike was writing it down in a neat row of Chinese characters.

"Thank you so much... and Helen, there is one more thing. It's kinda complicated to explain on the phone. When did you hire that assistant of yours?"

"Hmm... really. Why? Well, you won't like this next part. We are pretty sure she is not just working for you. When we left your place last time, Yau's men suddenly popped up out of nowhere. The only person who could have told them about us is her."

"Yeah... what can I say? I'm sorry to tell you like this, but I thought I do it rather sooner than later."

He listened for a while.

"I'm really, really sorry about this. I'll talk to Jia if she knows somebody good to replace her... Yeah, you too! Talk to you soon!"

He cut the connection and looked up over his shoulder at Dean with a pained expression. "Well, that was awkward."

43

KAREN SPENT THE afternoon napping in their cabin, completely exhausted from a nightlong hike and the excitement of what had happened in Huangshi.

The ship stopped several times at larger towns along the way, and every time Tseten left the cabin and wordlessly came back when the ship was moving again.

Late in the afternoon, Karen went out to watch the ship dock at another small port along the river, when she noticed several men in orange robes among the crowd on land. They stoically stood in the middle of a busy crowd, unmoving, only their eyes following the arriving vessel.

When the ship had been tied down, Tseten came out of the cabin and took up a position near the gangway to greet the orange robed monks coming aboard. Karen was intrigued. Was that what he had done all afternoon at the different stops? And indeed, now she could see two more monks on the deck above hers, leaning against the railing and also watching as the other monks came on board.

Tseten bowed to each of them deeply as he was by far the junior of them all. Only a few words were exchanged, and then the new arrivals went to an empty cabin on the same deck as Karen's. When their cabin door had closed, Tseten saw her watching him. He acknowledged her with a nod and came towards her.

"Tseten, are those friends of yours?"

He smiled solemnly. "Not friends. Masters."

THEY STOOD SIDE by side at the railing as the ship cast off again. As they moved away from shore, the setting sun appeared behind the buildings of the town in a red haze. Tall smokestacks were churning out smoke and steam that glowed orange-yellow in the evening light. The hulking shadows of other ships could be seen tied down along the waterfront. The air was still warm from the day and smelled of all the usual ship's smells – diesel oil, paint, rust, hydraulic fluids.

"So what are you and the other monks going to do when we come to Shanghai?"

"Rescue time."

She looked at him. He had turned very serious, staring at the sunset behind them. The last rays of the sun turned his face into a golden mask.

44

DEAN CAME OUT of the Suzhou Hotel and flagged down a taxi that had been waiting for customers not far from the entrance. The air was still hot from the day and little drops of sweat started forming on his forehead. He was wearing a jacket despite the heat since its inner pocket was the only way to carry the rolled up photographs with him without advertising the fact.

Mike and Jia had also put their new riches to work and had rented a Kevlar vest from a security company that Dean was now wearing under his shirt. It was heavy and hot and he already regretted that he had agreed to wearing it.

He gave the taxi driver the address of the Millennium Star Hotel construction site and he had to insist to go there when the taxi driver correctly pointed out to him that the place had not yet opened. The driver shrugged and joined the mayhem that passed for evening rush hour in this overcrowded city.

As always he was mesmerized by the view of Shanghai's waterfront at night, with all the buildings lit up by colorful floodlights. Traffic was slow and he had a lot of time to take it all in. The colonial palace-like buildings on the Bund side of the river, and the new skyscrapers praising the advent of the 21st century on the opposite side.

Traffic was faster near the airport and his mood turned to fear. Sooner than he wished they took an exit ramp and entered a dark labyrinth of unfinished office towers, construction pits, bumpy roads and a multitude of heavy machinery parked everywhere. After avoiding an epic pothole not unlike a bomb crater the taxi turned off the road altogether and stopped in a field of loose gravel.

THE DRIVER TURNED around and said "Millennium Star!" and pointed ahead at the dark tower in front of them. He clearly expected this clueless foreigner to get the hint and chose a different destination and he was baffled when Dean paid without a complaint.

Dean got out of the backseat with a grunt. "Thanks. Good night!" Dean slapped the door shut.

The taxi driver just stood there, not sure if he would be in trouble for leaving a tourist stranded out here. Dean went back and bent down to the open passenger window.

"It's OK. You can leave!" he tried a winning smile and gave the driver a cheerful thumbs-up to show that everything was hunky dory.

The driver still looked unsure, but finally shrugged and put the car into gear. He left and took most of the light with him. It was dark on the gravel field. The hotel actually had a few small red lights in long rows along the sides, probably to prevent helicopter pilots from getting the wrong idea about the availability of airspace.

THE GRAVEL WAS still giving back the heat it had received from the sun all day. The hot and humid air was unmoving and felt as thick as soup on his skin.

Dean stood in the middle of this dark space, slowly turning around and around. There were a few yellow Xenon lights along the road that passed the hotel, giving at least a little illumination. Dean could hear some heavy construction machines working in a deep pit several hundred yards away and occasionally a beam of light would shoot out from over there and light up the area around him for a split second at a time.

It was eleven o'clock.

Dean reached into his jacket pocket and hit the speed dial button on the phone Mike had given him. He stood still.

There was a faint sound of car engines, coming closer. He saw their lights bouncing up and down on the potholed street, and then they turned off the road and came straight at him. He had to raise an arm to prevent their lights from completely blinding him.

The two cars stopped next to each other, about thirty feet away from him. Doors opened, but he was still blinded by the lights and could only make out faint shadows backlit by the reflection of the car's red rear lights on the ground behind them. There were at least four people standing next to the cars. One of them seemed to be on a cell phone. Two more seemed to be holding guns.

The one to the very left slowly came towards him, walking past the front of the left car. Dean got a quick glimpse of his face before the man turned again into a complete shadow. He stopped about six feet away from Dean.

"GOOD EVENING, Mr. Lashure."

This was the smooth-talking British-accent guy. He had a good voice, Dean had to give him that.

"Where is Karen?"

"Oh. You are in a hurry, aren't you? We will first make sure that what you have brought us are the correct pictures. You did bring the photos?"

"I first want to see that you've brought Karen." Dean started sweating profusely.

The man shouted something in Chinese. The man on the very right opened the back door of the car and another shape appeared. It was the shape of a woman. The man held a gun to her head. Dean's heart was pumping so loud in his ears, it seemed to be about to burst. He wanted to run over there and hold her.

"Now let's see the pictures."

Dean nodded. He pulled the envelope with the prints from the inside pocket of his jacket. The man made a step towards him. Dean stepped back and held out a hand. They both stopped.

"Not yet. I will show you the pictures. And then I will put them on the ground between us and Karen will walk over to me. OK?"

"Very well."

He pulled the first picture out of the envelope. While he turned it around for the man to see, another beam of light from the construction machines behind Dean played across the field. He saw the girl's face and froze. He almost fell down with the shock. It was like a knife had been pushed into his stomach.

That was not Karen!

There would be no exchange. They would either take him or kill him, but at that moment all he could think about was what they had done to Karen. He bent down and put the picture on the ground with a badly shaking hand.

The man had not noticed what Dean had seen. Dean slowly pulled another photo from the envelope and turned it around. He had a few more moments to come up with a plan. He and Mike had never considered the possibility of them not having Karen with them. In hindsight, it had been pretty amateurish of them to be so optimistic about this situation.

While he bent down he hissed into his jacket. "No Karen."

"What?" The man pulled one leg back, narrowing his profile towards Dean.

"Oh... six more pictures." Dean pulled the next one from the envelope.

The man had become nervous. This took too long for his taste. "OK. We can see that you brought all of them. Just put the envelope down."

Dean had to play along for a little while longer. "When Karen starts walking towards me."

THE ARMED MAN next to the woman pushed her forward, towards him. She reluctantly walked a few steps, stumbled. It was obvious that she wanted to be nowhere close to Dean. He could hear the angry whine of a car engine coming closer. Chinese shouts between the men. The woman turned back to them and screamed something.

Dean dropped and picked the pictures off the ground. He jumped back up and tried to run towards the side of the cars. His feet slipped on the gravel. The smooth-talker shouted orders. Dean changed direction and tackled the man with his right shoulder. He heard rips snap with a satisfying crack.

A Toyota pickup was bouncing onto the gravel field, lights blazing. It stopped in a bow wave of gravel as its tires found purchase. Four men jumped off the open truck bed. They pulled weapons from their shoulder holsters.

Yau's men understood the situation instinctively. They crammed into the cars. One of the cars jumped forward. It stopped next to the pile of Dean and the smooth-talker. Dean saw a gun facing his way. It was a strangely abstract moment. He had time to see every intricate detail of the gun, the oily darkness of its muzzle. There was a flash and his breast filled with pain. Smoke. It burned his face and the acrid smell of fireworks was all around him. Darkness fell.

MIKE WAS BEHIND the wheel of the pickup and he heard the shot through his earpiece first and then through the open window. His blood froze. The two black cars sped up, wildly fishtailing before they made it out of the gravel lot and onto the street.

They left behind the small heap of a human figure on the ground. The four men Mike had hired ran over to the body. Mike opened the door of the truck with violently shaking hands and walked unsteadily behind them.

When he arrived next to Dean's lifeless body, the four bodyguards had already peeled back the jacket and were about to rip off the shirt. There was no blood. They took the shirt off completely and lifted the Kevlar vest Dean had been so reluctant to wear.

Two of the guards made appreciative remarks about the vest. It had stopped the bullet. A palm-sized, dark blue bruise was forming in the upper right area of Dean's breast just below the collar bone.

One of the men had been monitoring Deans pulse at his neck. He now pulled a small plastic tube from a wallet-sized first-aid kit and broke it under Dean's nose.

Dean's body convulsed. He coughed. His eyes fluttered open. He gasped for air and pressed his left hand against the bruise on his breast.

"WELCOME BACK, BUDDY!"

"Ouch!" Dean whispered. He gasped for air. This was hurting a lot more than any other injury he had ever had. His whole breast was a pulsing nerve ending, sending a scream of pain up his spine.

The four men slowly helped him up, first to a sitting position and then to a unsteady stumble. They helped him back to the pickup. One of the men had called their driver, and now another vehicle arrived in the gravel lot, a gray SUV with a large steel fender.

They helped Dean into the Toyota pickup and their leader came over to Mike's window. He was a broad-shouldered, tanned man in his late forties, with startlingly blue eyes and a military haircut. He stood there straight-backed, almost at attention.

"SIR, IT IS my understanding that our engagement for tonight is over. Is that correct?"

"Yes. Thank you very much. Do I have to sign something?"

"No. Most of our clients appreciate the absence of paperwork. Thank you for doing business with us. You have the 24-hour number for Shanghai Security Associates?"

"Yes. We may have a follow-up engagement."

"So it seems. Call us anytime. Good Luck." He saluted and then he paused. He scanned the surroundings in a quick motion. "We will drive behind you until we hit the highway. Consider that a free service for a first-time customer." The man saluted quickly and walked back around the pickup to their SUV.

Mike turned back to Dean, who looked like he needed a drink, a massage, and a bed, all at the same time. "You OK?"

"I'm hurting all over. And they didn't bring Karen back. So... no, not really. Oh – and they have the photos. It's a bit late today, but I expect them in the Suzhou Hotel by tomorrow morning." He let his head fall back.

45

WHEN MIKE AND Dean had left for the airport, Jia didn't want to stay alone in the Suzhou Hotel. She took the little red car across town to her uncle's warehouse where she could always help him with organizing the liquidation of their gold.

She was driving into the parking lot in front of the warehouse, when she had to swerve sharply to avoid being rammed by the truck they had used last night for transporting the gold. She looked up and saw her cousin Zhou and another figure waving at her cheerfully.

She parked next to the huge loading door and walked into the warehouse.

One of the workers who had been with her uncle for years greeted her with a big smile. "Zhou is going for it again, eh?"

She looked at him baffled. "What?"

The worker looked unsure if he had maybe said too much.

"He's... going to get more gold, isn't he?"

Jia stood there, thunderstruck. For several moments, she did not move at all. Then, very quiet, she asked. "What did he tell you?"

"He said that he and Kun – you know Kun? - would go back to the hotel to... clean up?" The man was taking a step backwards when he saw her face.

JIA'S FACE HAD turned red. Her mouth opened, but no sound came out. She turned and ran to the offices in the corner of the building.

She slammed the door open. Her uncle was bent down over a stack of papers, making notes along the sides. He looked up and smiled at her briefly until he had seen her face. "What is going on?"

"That's my question to you! Zhou went back to the hotel? Are you nuts?"

Her uncle's face went through a remarkable series of emotions. He turned white. Then red.

"What?"

"I just talked to your man out there. He says that Zhou went to 'clean up'. With Kun."

By the time she had finished the sentence, her uncle had already run past her to interrogate the worker.

Jia looked at her watch. It was too late to call Mike – they were already meeting with Yau's men. Maybe she could catch up with Zhou and Kun before they got to the roof of the Suzhou Hotel. She ran out to where she had parked and seconds later the little red car came screaming out of the parking lot.

On the way back through Shanghai's downtown area she tried to call Mike anyway, but his cell phone was off. She left a message and pushed the car to its limits to get to the hotel before her cousin could do anything stupid.

46

THEY DROVE BACK into the city in silence, Dean resting with his eyes closed and his left hand over the bruise under his shoulder. It was after midnight when they arrived at the warehouse of Jia's uncle. They parked out front and entered the place through a small, rusty side-door. The uncle stood on the loading dock screaming at one of his men. He stopped abruptly when he saw Mike and Dean approaching.

He jumped from the dock and came over to the two men. He started talking to Mike when he was still thirty feet away, his words coming out in machine gun-like spurts. He pointed back at the man he had chewed out before and his voice was rising again to give him another piece of his mind across the length of the warehouse.

Mike barely managed to put in a question sideways. Suddenly he stepped back. Dean understood "Jia" and "Suzhou Fandian" and a dark foreboding crept into his mind. Mike turned back to him.

"Fuck! Zhou... you know, Jia's idiot cousin? Zhou got it into his head that he could take the rest of the gold! He and one of his buddies took the truck back to the Suzhou Hotel and when Jia heard about it she went there to stop them!"

Dean looked at the other man. "What about him?"

"Oh he let Zhou take the truck and didn't say anything until later."

"When did they leave?"

"About half an hour ago. And Jia left just after them!" Mike was on his way back out.

Dean followed. "Oh shit. You realize who could be joining that party?"

THEY WERE BACK at the pickup. Mike was fumbling with the keys in the door lock. "Yep. And I want Jia out of there."

Mike drove the truck like a madman. They pushed through a dark industrial neighborhood and up a ramp onto one of the new ring highways that circled all of Shanghai.

With one hand he was operating his cell phone. "Shitshitshit. Jia's phone is off." He held the phone to his head. "Hey sweetie! If you are still in the Suzhou Hotel, get the hell out of there. Forget about your cousin. Just leave. Yau's men have the photos and they'll be over there as soon as they look at the pictures and see the streaks on the carpet in room 517. Get out now!"

He snapped his phone shut. "I'm an idiot. She even left me a message, but guess what, I forgot to check after we got away from the Millennium Star."

47

AT THE HOTEL Jia first checked the dark alley around the corner. The truck was parked where it had been standing the day before. There was nobody there and all she could hear was the slow ticking of the engine cooling down. She turned and sprinted to the main entrance, only slowing down inside to casually stroll past the reception desk.

Jia ran up the stairs as fast as she could and then on the fifth floor she changed to the utility stairs. The lock of the door to the roof had been broken. It had not been done with any finesse whatsoever, her cousin had simply used a crowbar.

She walked out onto the roof, still warm from the heat of the day. It was midnight and a slim moon was low over the horizon. There was not much light and she had to wait for a little while until her eyes adjusted to the darkness. She only heard her own breathing, still fast from running up the stairs. She leaned against the wall next to the open door.

THEN SHE HEARD it. A low humming noise that made every atom in her body dance. She was sliding along the wall and sat down hard on the concrete floor. It felt like her body kept on falling, her mind was free floating above it. She saw herself sitting on the floor. Everything slowed down.

Strange yellow lights danced in the air to her left, but they suddenly dimmed down again and disappeared. She felt in control of her body again. She slowly got up and walked along the iron grating back to the chimney that led to room 517. A strong rope had been tied around a neighboring chimney and was running taut to the edge and down to the secret door. She looked down into the chimney and saw light streaming from the small door, maybe fifteen feet down.

She was afraid to shout, but she managed a loud hiss. "Zhou! Are you down there?"

A face appeared at the door. "He's down here. Is that you, Jia?"

"Kun? What the hell are you doing here? Did Zhou get you involved in this?"

"Of course. Listen... This is a scary place! There's a fucking skeleton down here!" His eyes were big.

"And just now something strange happened. We opened this box, and Zhou took out some sort of golden ball... and suddenly all hell broke loose down here. Zhou is unconscious and I haven't been able to wake him up."

"You have to get the hell out of there! You two are completely out of your mind! There's a good chance that a bunch of Hong Kong Triad men are going to come here! Tonight!"

Kun had not needed another reason to panic. His head disappeared in a hurry. Jia could still hear his voice. "Come on! Zhou! Wake up! Wakeupwakeupwakeup! Damnit!"

Kun's head reappeared. "Listen. He's completely out. I'll tie him up with the rope and we can pull him out!"

Jia mumbled to herself. "Tie it around his neck! What an idiot!"

A SHORT WHILE later Kun appeared again. He pulled himself through the door, paused a moment to arrange something heavy at the entrance to the attic and then he climbed up the rope. He was pretty nimble on the rope and his head appeared at the chimney opening after only a few seconds. He was face to face with Jia. She hissed at him. "Was this his idea?"

"Of course." Kun pulled himself out of the chimney and jumped down onto the roof. He was wearing black pants and a black t-shirt, both covered in gray dust. "You know Zhou. Any get-rich-quick scheme and he is sold."

"And so why did you come along?"

"What can I say. I was drunk when I agreed. It did sound pretty good at the time." He gave Jia his flashlight.

Kun went back up on the chimney and stood with one leg on each side of it. He bent down, picked up the rope and started to pull. Jia held the flashlight down into the chimney. Suddenly she saw Zhou's head appear at the door opening. Then she could see his upper body with the rope tied around his breast under the arms. Kun had to pull hard and almost slipped on the thin brick edge of the chimney. Zhou slowly made his unconscious trip back to the world of the living, with Kun breathing hard with every pull.

As Zhou's body appeared at the edge of the chimney, Jia pulled his arms over the side and held onto them. Kun grabbed the rope at the loop around Zhou's breast and pulled him all the way up. Now Jia could grab his legs and pull them out of the chimney altogether. Kun was breathing hard and slowly lowered Zhou down to the roof. At that moment a new light appeared under him in the chimney. Kun looked down. A bright light shone up from down at the fireplace. He heard a man shout something in Cantonese. He let go of Zhou and jumped off the chimney.

Jia was kneeling next to Zhou and looked up at Kun. "What was that?"

Kun whispered back. "There's somebody down in the room with the fireplace. I thought Zhou said it was blocked off!"

Jia's eyes turned big. "Not anymore. Did they see you?"

"I don't know. He was shouting something in Cantonese."

AT THAT MOMENT the beam of a flashlight hit them from the door to the roof. Two men came running along the iron grates. Jia tried to make herself as small as possible.

A voice shouted in English. "Jia! Are you OK?"

Kun jumped up and asked in Chinese. "Who is that?"

Jia in Chinese. "Be quiet!" In English. "Be quiet!"

Mike and Dean came up to them, both of them out of breath. Mike kneeled down to look at Zhou.

"There's men down in room 517! They've removed the cover from the fireplace!"

Mike covered his flashlight and switched it off. Dean stood behind him with his hands on his knees, still completely out of breath. Sweat was dripping off his nose. It had been an exhausting evening for him and it was still hot and humid.

"What's up with Zhou?" Mike whispered.

"The idiot spun one of the spheres. He's been unconscious ever since. Kun had to pull him out of the chimney on a rope."

Mike switched to Chinese for Kun. "Can you carry Zhou down the utility stairs? It's too narrow for two to carry him."

"Maybe. He's pretty heavy for such a thin kid. I'll try."

"Let's go." he switched to English. "Dean, they are already down in room 517. Let's get out of here."

"Swell. I'll never again buy a camera on eBay!"

CARRYING A LIFELESS body is not as easy as one would think. Mike had a moment to reflect on this as they tried to get Zhou to the roof door. At the end Mike just threw him over his shoulder and carried him alone. At the door, Kun took over and they followed Dean down the narrow stairs.

Dean suddenly stopped. He almost fell when Kun with Zhou on his shoulder bumped into him.

"Mr. Lashure! What a surprise. I thought we had seen the last of each other."

48

KAREN WOKE TO the noise of the cabin door opening. It was still dark outside and Karen couldn't see much. The floor lights from the walkway along the outside of the cabins showed her the shapes of two monks talking. One of them must have been Tseten. She looked at her watch. It was just after midnight.

The discussion between the monks was intense. Something must have happened, but Karen had no idea how they would have gotten any news. They were in the middle of the Yangtze river, almost half a mile from the nearest shore.

Then she remembered what the monk in the temple garden in Shanghai had said just before he got shot. He had said that they could somehow sense when somebody was manipulating the spheres. So maybe another one of the spheres in the attic had become active. That was interesting.

Tseten came back into the cabin and closed the door. It was completely dark. She could only hear his bare feet touch the metal bars of the ladder as he climbed into his bunk above hers, but there was no noticeable vibration. How did he do that?

"Tseten?"

"Sorry for waking you!"

"No. It's OK. Did something happen?"

"Yes. We... do not know. But something happen. We can feel."

KAREN KNEW THAT there was not much more she would be able to get out of him. She leaned back into her bunk, again regretting the she and Tseten had no better way to communicate.

The bed was surprisingly comfortable, but it was a very hot night. She pulled the thin sheet she was using as a blanket up to her chin and tried to relax.

But questions kept on bubbling to the surface of her consciousness. How was Dean? Were they trying to find her? Were they in danger?

She had been thinking all day of a way to let them know that she was safe, but now she was stuck on a boat, in the middle of the widest river she had ever seen... sometimes they could only see one of the banks as the other bank of the river had disappeared over the horizon.

She was still exhausted from the last couple of days and the slight motion of the ship finally made her doze off again. Soon she fell into a deep, dreamless sleep.

The ship was gliding through the night on water smooth as glass, with only the regular sound of its deep bass horn breaking the silence on the river.

49

THE OFFICE HAD desks along the windows with additional tables protruding into the room. Stacks of travel brochures on the tables leaned dangerously. Several yellowed posters picturing ShanghaiTrans planes above the clouds were tacked to the walls. The computers on the desks showed a screensaver with little animated ShanghaiTrans airplanes rushing across a map of China.

There was a small fridge next to the entrance, a coat rack and several mismatched chairs for visitors to sit on. A heavy file cabinet had been dragged away from the old fireplace, revealing the white brickwork, the ironworks, and the empty fire pit.

Dean, Jia, Mike, Kun and Zhou were sitting along the back wall of suite 517, all of them with their hands bound with plastic handcuffs. Zhou was still unconscious.

THE SMOOTH-TALKING GUY had been only the first of four blue-suited men, all of them heavily armed. There had been no resistance. Dean remembered only too well that only one hour ago they had left him for dead with a bullet stuck in his Kevlar vest. The only thing giving Dean any solace was the fact that the smoothtalker was holding his right side most of the time. Dean's shoulder must have done quite some damage.

There had been no interrogation. Yau's men were satisfied that they knew everything they needed to know.

Two men stood guard over them at all times. One other man had come in later and had given them water bottles. He had checked on Zhou's pulse, but had done nothing else for him.

They all were dozing. Jia had her head propped up on Mike's shoulder. Dean was intensely uncomfortable with his bruise from the bullet, but he didn't think he would get any sympathy from this crowd. As far as he could tell, one of the men guarding him right now had been the man behind the gun. When he closed his eyes he could still see the muzzle flash.

WHEN DEAN OPENED his eyes next, the sun had come up. The sky was overcast and it was already very humid. Through the open window he could hear the sounds of Shanghai waking up. The clock on the wall said it was half past seven. His back hurt and his bruised right shoulder had lost all feeling, which he considered a good thing.

Dean looked around. Zhou was stretched out on the floor, his breast slowly rising and falling. Mike had slipped down along the wall, with his head in a steep angle to his body, snoring loudly. Jia had her head up against his breast and right arm, sleeping soundly. Kun looked back at Dean and nodded. Different guards stood now at the two ends of the row of prisoners.

He leaned back again and closed his eyes. It was better to be rested for whatever was coming their way. He concentrated on the sounds he could hear through the open windows. There were boat horns and the incessant tucktucktuck of the open engines on the small freight boats. He could hear car horns and bicyclists talking to each other on the road past the hotel. It all sounded very peaceful and he soon dozed off again.

DEAN WOKE UP again. He rubbed his eyes awkwardly with his tied hands. When he looked up, the smoothtalker walked into the room. But he immediately stopped, turned around and bowed, gesturing for somebody else to enter.

An old man entered the room. Dean realized that he was looking at Martin Yau. The man was now at least ninety years old, but he held his body like he was working out daily. Dean would have guessed him at mid-sixty, if he wouldn't have known his true age.

He was of average height, had a lean body and an oval, clear face. His eyes were two black, polished coals. When he came closer, Dean could see that he had hundreds of thin wrinkles in his tanned face that did not register across a room. He walked like he owned the world.

Another man had entered the office. He was tanned, in his mid-forties, with a muscular body. He was wearing a dark suit and had sunglasses in his hair. He walked past the old man with aggressive steps and stopped in front of Dean.

"So you are Lashure?" His voice was high-pitched.

Dean just looked at him.

"So you think that I'm not worth talking to, yes? Well, your girlfriend was more talkative. In fact, she was very... flexible."

Dean's heart stopped. And beat again, faster. This man had interrogated Karen. Torture? His face flushed. He pulled his right leg in.

The man stepped back. "Want to kick me?" He flashed a toothy smile, but his eyes were completely cold. He stepped forward and gave Dean a vicious kick against his right shoulder. Exactly above the spot the bullet had hit last night. Dean jerked back and hit his head against the wall. His body was engulfed in a wave of pain.

"You will never again stand in the way of my father!"

MARTIN YAU SAID something in a steely voice. His son turned around and walked towards the other end of the room, looking out the window.

Martin Yau examined the room, his quick eyes not missing a thing. He inspected the fireplace, took a flashlight from the top of the file cabinet and leaned into the chimney. He came back out with a quick smile on his face. It disappeared immediately when he turned around and looked at the prisoners on the ground.

By now Mike had woken up and had shaken Jia awake. Both were now sitting up. Kun seemingly had not moved since Dean had seen him several hours ago. Zhou was still out – whatever he had done with the sphere, his body had not liked it.

The smoothtalker walked up next to Martin Yau and pointed at each of the prisoners, seemingly whispering a short biography into Yau's ear for each of them. Dean was last and Yau got a very long story about him. Yau's eyes were fixed on Dean the whole time and that look made Dean very uneasy.

Several other people of Yau's entourage had shown up and he and his people held a meeting at the other end of the room, the prisoners momentarily forgotten. He seemed to be a busy man. He made a number of phone calls and he wrote several notes that he passed to men who ran out of the room. Nobody even acknowledged the presence of the handcuffed prisoners against the other wall. It seemed to Dean that this was par for the course for his employees.

Some time later a very athletic young man entered the room and after a quick talk to Yau started to attack the chimney. He pretty much freeclimbed up into it and had reached the door in a few minutes. While he was looking around in the attic, he gave a running report on a cell phone to Yau, who looked very pleased to Dean's eyes. Yau had been waiting for this day for more than five decades.

IT HAD BECOME lunch time, but all the prisoners got was a bathroom break. Each one of them was led to the bathroom by one of the guards and there handcuffs were cut, just to be replaced with new ones when they came back out. While this went on, Yau and his son had left, presumably for a celebratory lunch, now that he had the gold back.

Several more men showed up and together with the one man up in the attic they installed a rope and pulley system in the chimney very similar to the one Mike and Dean had used. It seemed as if Yau didn't want to lose any time about getting the treasure out of the hotel.

WHILE ALL THIS went on, Dean had a chance to talk to Mike in whispers.

"What the hell is he planning to do with us?"

Mike shrugged. "No idea. They talk Cantonese with each other and my Cantonese is not even enough to order a hamburger down in Hong Kong."

"I have a feeling they are just waiting for nightfall. Once it is dark and reasonable quiet around the hotel, they'll try and get us out of here." He gave Mike a significant look.

Mike nodded. "Yeah, I'm afraid so, too. I didn't like the look on Yau's face when he was talking to his people. At one point he was clearly giving them instructions on what to do... with us."

50

THEIR SHIP HAD reached the delta of the Yangtze river, and all signs of land had disappeared in the humid haze. The water was still dark yellow from the sediment of the river, but the waves had turned choppy and signaled how close they were to the open ocean.

Everywhere on the boat Karen could now see the monks in their orange robes. Many of them must have been traveling from all over China to join this boat, but she never saw any luggage. They all just seemed to have a small leather pouch under the robes for some money and maybe a small book, but no other earthly possessions weighed them down.

Groups of monks were talking above decks, and Karen had many free hours during the day to watch them, like the remaining passengers did. Sometimes the monks were laughing and joking, especially when long lost friends seemed to meet. But most of the conversations were very solemn and led with concentration.

Something big was happening that brought all the Guardians of Time to Shanghai, and by now Karen had a pretty good idea what that was.

THE DAY HAD already turned to evening when the ship entered the mouth of the Pujiang river. There was dense traffic on the water and the horn of their ship gave regular signals. Karen stood at the bow and willed the ship forward. A light wind had come up and blew her hair back. It did not provide much relief against the humid heat. It had been a lightly overcast day with the sun visible as an undefined, unbearably bright splotch in the white sky.

They passed under several large suspension bridges, and the colossal TV tower at the tip of Pudong with its round, bubble-shaped viewing platforms and restaurants came into view, already lit up for the night in a thousand shades of pink.

The ship slowed down and veered to starboard. Karen could see where they would be docking and it was only maybe half a mile from the Suzhou Hotel. In fact, she could actually see the squat, dark gray building of the hotel between several higher and more modern buildings. Dean would be there!

TSETEN CAME UP behind her. She reluctantly turned away from the view and looked at him. He still looked like a teenager in a robe several numbers too big. But she had seen how strong he was, both physically and mentally. He had rescued her, protected her, had actually fought for her and killed two men in the process. She looked in his eyes and shuddered.

"I... I don't even know what to say. Thank you! Thank you so much for rescuing me..." She held up her arms to embrace him.

"We go there." He raised one arm past her shoulder. She knew he was pointing exactly in the direction she had been looking at. He was pointing at the Suzhou Hotel.

She dropped her arms to her sides. "Me too."

For the first time through all their adventures, Tseten looked surprised. "There? Why?"

"That's where my man is."

<h1 style="text-align:center">51</h1>

ANOTHER BOX ARRIVED in the fire pit. For more than an hour now, boxes came out of the chimney at a rate of one every two minutes. Several large stacks of the boxes had started to fill one corner of the office. With all the activity their guards had become less attentive and Mike and Dean were whispering to each other.

"Mike, have you noticed that they are only bringing down the small boxes with the spheres?"

"Yeah, that's why they are so fast. Once they get to the gold bars, they'll slow down. Each of the gold boxes weighs about forty pounds. That will take them all night."

"It's almost dark already." Dean nodded at the window.

Mike turned his head to take a look. "Strange. It's a bit early. But look at those clouds! There's going to be a thunderstorm later tonight. You could feel it coming all day. What do you think, how much more time do we have?"

"When Yau is back, I guess we are going to be the first item on his agenda."

Mike looked at the door and back at Dean. He sighed. "Well, speak of the devil."

THE MEN WHO were sorting the boxes interrupted their work. All the prisoners looked up, with the exception of Zhou who had been completely out since the night before. Kun had been trying to give him water, but without a doctor there was not much else they could do.

Yau looked at the stacks of boxes and gave the men an appreciative nod. They started their work again, but a sharp question from Yau made them all stand up as if they were puppets and he had pulled their strings. He slowly knelt down next to the boxes and looked at them closer. One of the men talked to him in an apologetic tone.

The other one pulled a cell phone from his pocket and dialed. When he got an answer, he gave the phone to Martin Yau.

Mike leaned over to Dean and hissed. "He's calling the guy in the attic!"

Yau, still on one knee next to the boxes, was talking into the phone while looking at the ceiling. He seemed to be agitated.

"I think I know what he is looking for." Dean hissed back at Mike.

"Oh. The... ghost... that I saw screwed him over?"

"Exactly. I'm wondering now, what is in that box? We never opened it."

"Still in your room?"

One of the guards looked at them threateningly.

Mike gave Dean a slow nod and they leaned back again.

ALL THE WHILE Yau had been talking to the man in the attic, alternatively instructing and berating him. His face was flushed and he looked angry and tired at the same time.

Dean heard distant thunder rolling across the lead-colored sky. Again, louder this time.

Finally Martin Yau closed the phone, placed it on one of the boxes and got up. He slowly came over to the row of prisoners along the wall when his son strode into the room. The young man did not look at anybody, but had his eyes on the ground, moving in a smooth arc over to where his father was. He arrived in front of the prisoners at the same time as Martin Yau.

The father turned his head and looked at his son. Dean could now see that there was indeed a family relationship. They both had the same eyes and chin. But where the father was cold and calculating, the son was hotblooded and short-tempered.

Dean's thoughts were interrupted by the appearance of a gun in the son's right hand.

His heart skipped a beat.

IT WAS A heavy, metal-gray automatic weapon with a silencer attached. It had appeared in the hands of Yau's son as if by magic.

Dean could not stop staring at the muzzle of the silencer. That small black circle was not even pencil-thick and looked so insignificant, so insubstantial, it appeared not even to be a real hole in the metal of the gun. But Dean had seen last night how fire and metal could spring from such a tiny opening to spread pain and death.

Martin Yau said a word in Cantonese and his son nodded and tried to say something in response, but his father cut him off with a quick movement of his hand. Now the father turned back to the prisoners.

"Have you been removing items from the attic?" It was the first time they had heard him speak in English.

Dean decided to try some half-truths first. "We have been in there, but had no time to do anything since our friend over there had that accident. And then your men showed up." He pointed at the unconscious Zhou, stretched out on the ground.

"I am looking for one specific box. If you return it to me, I will spare your lives." He was almost pleading with them.

Dean decided that telling him would do no good. Yau was not known for sparing lives. "Sorry, but I don't know what you are talking about."

"HE IS LYING. They are all lying!" The son was frustrated. He pointed the gun at Mike. Then at Jia. Over to Kun. He turned his head without removing his eyes from the prisoners. "Dad, look at this!" With his free hand he pulled a room key for the Suzhou Hotel from his jacket pocket. He held it up high.

"I found this among the things we took from them." His face turned back and he stared at Dean. "You are staying in this hotel and you for sure did not check in last night when we caught you here!"

He dropped the key into his father's open hand and flashed his shark smile at the prisoners. "This was not the first time you went into the attic. One of you is going to tell us what we want to know. Or I'll just shoot somebody first, how about that?"

There was more thunder outside. The air was charged with electricity and a sudden gust of cool air came through the windows, billowing the curtains.

The son smiled with a nervous tick while his eyes jumped left and right. He knew he had their full attention and he swung the gun back and forward, watching them intently. His father said something in a sharp tone of voice. The son answered angrily and lowered his gun again. He turned back to the prisoners. "So which one should I shoot first?" His eyes were glowing and small droplets of sweat stood on his forehead.

The prisoners in front of him did not dare to breathe.

"Maybe her." The gun snapped back up and pointed at Jia. She gasped and closed her eyes. Her head bumped back against the wall.

"No!" Mike screamed. His face had changed completely, with his teeth showing and his eyes all white, like a cornered animal.

Yau's son swung the gun at Mike's head. Then over to Dean. Back to Mike.

"Yes, maybe you first. You are Japanese. You know what they did to us during the war?"

Mike was breathing hard. There was blood dripping from his wrists where the plastic handcuffs had cut into his skin.

"You idiot! He is American, not Japanese." Jia spat the words at him.

"Ah... not much better..."

MARTIN YAU HAD enough. "Too much talk!" He took the gun from his son's hand, checked the safety switch in a fluid, well-trained motion and pointed it back at Dean.

Dean took what he thought would be his last breath.

THERE WAS A loud crack. Yau and his son looked over their shoulders. Dean's eyes refocused on the world.

One of the small boxes had slipped from the ropes and had dropped into the fireplace. It had broken and a golden sphere had been catapulted into the room. Dean's eyes caught the golden glitter of the polished sphere as it described a small, low arc over the ironworks of the fireplace. It landed with a dull thud on the wooden floor and started rolling. It's inner spheres turned.

There was a metallic hum.

THE WORLD AROUND them lost all color and dimmed.

Dean could hear only his own breathing in his ears. His hairs stood up. The wall behind his back turned inward and the floor fell away. Everything was slowing down and his heart beat like a drum in his breast. He rolled forward and willed his legs to push.

Mike already had one leg under him when the sphere dropped. He jumped. His mind and body separated and he saw his own body fly against Yau's son. There was a loud crunching noise vibrating up through his body, but no other sound could be heard.

Jia felt like she was weightless. She saw the sphere rolling along, slowing down... *turning back!* Kun's body was suddenly in the way, but he did not look real, he was... blurry.

Kun had also jumped up. He had been ready for a final desperate assault. He had already started to get up when the sphere suddenly appeared. His jump was a strange, quiet flight through the air. It seemed to take minutes before he hit the closest of the two guards.

BOTH GUARDS HAD reacted to the crack of the box. They had turned around in an instant and where in the middle of pulling their guns when time splintered into a thousand realities. Their momentum carried them forward, away from the prisoners now behind them.

The golden ball danced in front of their feet. Strange forces were pulling at their bodies. All light around them seemed to get sucked into the sphere as it glowed with a golden fire.

MARTIN YAU INSTINCTIVELY pulled the trigger. The gun became hot in his hand and a growing, perfect ball of smoke enveloped his lower arm. There was a dull pain. His eyesight narrowed to a tunnel of golden light. He tried to scream for his guards, but no sounds came out of his mouth.

His age-old instincts took over, like they had so many times in his life. He started to turn and run towards the open connecting door to the neighboring room.

YAU'S SON HAD no chance to even look back. Something was ramming into his body, pressing all the air out of his lungs. Something snapped. Suddenly he could see himself from the outside, bent in an unnatural angle with Mike pushing against him.

The sphere left a trace of burnt wood in its track. It was slowly dancing back and forward in small loops. The sound emanating from it had turned more and more menacing as several of its inner spheres spun up, one after another. It was now an angry roar.

The men who had been stacking the boxes tried to jump back, away from the screaming sphere. Their legs did not work properly and their vision was distorted. They both stumbled against the stacks and several boxes tumbled down. Still in midflight, one of the boxes emitted another haunting, humming noise.

A terrible scream could be heard from the attic above.

52

THERE WERE SO many of them. Karen had never seen more than four or five monks at any given time on the boat, but now they all had come down the gangway, and Karen was astonished by the spectacle in front of her.

There must have been more than thirty monks, all of them in flowing orange robes that seemed to glow from within before a background of thunderstorm clouds. The air all around her seemed to be charged with electricity and the smell of summer rain hung in the air.

Other passengers still on the boat were leaning against the railing, chattering with each other and pointing at the monks. There was nervous laughter and calls to the departing monks with questions that stayed unanswered.

A single policeman stood on the dockside with his hands behind his back, keeping a watchful eye on the monks, but doing nothing. He was older and had the look of a man who had seen it all before, who was not going to get himself in trouble just because a bunch of monks arrived on a boat.

THE MONKS WALKED away from the boat dock in small groups, mostly using side streets, but all of them converging on the Suzhou Hotel only about half a mile away. Karen stayed with the group that Tseten had joined and the other monks didn't seem to mind.

She could hear thunder over the city. There was a glimmer of lightning behind clouds above the metropolis, far beyond the downtown area. There was more thunder.

The monks walked with what looked like slow, deliberate steps, but Karen had a hard time keeping up with them. She practically had to jog to stay alongside her group. Only once did Tseten look over to her and his face lit up for a short, encouraging smile, before he turned back to look at the dark gray building of the Suzhou Hotel in front of them.

One of the orange robed figures was waiting at a small side entrance of the hotel, not more than an emergency exit. The Guardians of Time arrived and they entered the building, one by one.

Tseten held Karen back and they entered the hotel together as the last ones. They found themselves at the foot of a utility stairwell and Karen guessed that it had to be the same one Dean had shown her when they had checked in. These stairs went all the way to the roof of the hotel.

Karen was shivering, but she did not know if from excitement or from a drop in temperature. She whispered to Tseten. "I know where the boxes are!"

He nodded. "We know. Tonight we..." His whole body jerked back and the cape fell from his shaven head, revealing his face.

KAREN HAD NEVER seen such a look of shock before. His pupils turned upwards and she saw only white in his eyes. She heard sighs and monks stumbling on the stairs above.

And then she felt it, too. A falling sensation, not very strong, and the faint realization that colors around her were fading...

She knew what this meant. Somebody had spun one of the spheres.

The lights were dimming, flickering. Tseten started running, flying up the stairs, barely touching the ground between jumps. Karen tried to keep up and was running up the stairs two steps at a time, but soon she was alone in the stairwell.

DEAN WAS ABOUT to kick Yau's legs from under him when the gun exploded in front of his face. Yau had pulled the trigger and after a brief flash a growing cloud of smoke enveloped his hand. Dean's legs connected with Yau's while he stared at the cloud. Small metal shrapnel was coming out of the smoke, with one large piece coming close to hit him. He tried to dodge it by diving under Yau's body as the old man started to fall over him.

There was a sharp pain as the shrapnel of the gun scraped along his scull. Yau was not falling as he had thought. The old man brought his other foot forward to change his fall into forward momentum. Dean became aware of sounds. There was now a hum in the air that drowned out everything else. It came from everywhere and vibrated along the bones in Dean's body. All around him where bodies in motion. Everything was strange – too fast, too slow, the perspective constantly shifting in and out of his body.

Suddenly there was a new color. Orange.

THE SHAPES ENTERED the room, just an orange blur. Dean thought of the strange apparitions they had encountered in the attic above this room and he squinted to resolve them better. And suddenly he understood. The Guardians of Time had arrived.

MIKE FELL HEADLONG to the ground. He couldn't see clearly, but he noticed Martin Yau jumping past him with Dean sliding along the wooden floor under the old man. There was smoke everywhere. Did Yau shoot? All he could hear was the humming of the spheres – all of them seemed to have joined in the resonating chorus, golden spheres singing out to their unknown creators. One sphere had been bad enough, but with all of them going off, what were the consequences? They'd have a lot of explaining to do if they made it out of there alive.

Mike turned and saw the young Yau falling on to the first sphere which by now had burned a blackened path into the hardwood floor. When his face touched the sphere there was a flash of fire. The sphere bounced away and Yau rolled himself in the other direction. Mike could hear his high-pitched scream over the hum of the spheres. The smell of burnt flesh and gunpowder stung his nostrils.

THERE WAS AN orange shape looming over Mike, in stark contrast to the washed-out colors of the rest of the room. He held up his arms to protect himself and the shape grabbed his arms and pulled him up. There were now more of these shapes... monks? He remembered now Karen and Dean's encounter with an orange-clad monk. Where did they all suddenly come from?

The hum was slowly subsiding, but still strong. Dean could see clear again. He took his first breath in what seemed like hours. Yau's son was rolling on the floor screaming. There was smoke coming off his face. His father had disappeared through the door, leaving a trail of blood from what was left of his right hand.

One of the bodyguards was kneeling on the ground, wrestling with Kun for control of the gun in his hands. Kun hit the guard's temple with his elbow and the man went limp.

The other bodyguard pulled his gun up and aimed at one of the monks. Time fractured again. There was suddenly a monk crouching next to the bodyguard who was falling to the ground, unconscious or dead.

Dean pushed himself up, but his arms and legs were unsteady and he almost fell over again. Color returned to the world around them. The humming slowed even further. He turned and pulled Mike onto his feet. They leaned on each other.

"DEAN!" THE SOUND of the voice whipped him around.

"Karen!" His own voice sounded strange to him.

There she was! She had stopped in the doorway and now she came running towards him.

There was a scream from next to the desks at the window. Yau's son jumped forward and grabbed the gun from the fallen guard. He pulled it up and aimed at Karen, his face a burned mask of hatred. Karen jumped back, more because of the spectacle of his face than the gun.

There was another motion too fast for Dean's eyes. Time split again. One moment Yau's body had been arching up, holding a gun, and only a blink of an eye later, he was on the ground, his lifeless face a burnt, bloody mess.

A young monk, still a teenager stood next to him as if he had always been there, legs wide, arms hanging loosely down the sides. There was blood on his shoe. The gun clattered to a stop next to his feet. He looked back at Karen gave her a slow nod. His cape had fallen back and the robe had opened over his breast where a large, round tattoo was now visible.

KAREN WALKED UP to the monk. "Thank you, Tseten!" She hugged him for a moment and then she turned to Dean, who by now had managed to stand on his own.

They looked at each other. Karen's tan had deepened over the last few days. She looked beautiful. Dean on the other hand looked like he needed sleep. A lot of sleep. There was blood slowly dripping down from his right temple. His face was white with dark rings around his eyes and his chin was stubbly.

She slowly walked over to him and they hugged.

MIKE WAS LEANING against the frame of the connecting door. He had a small trickle of blood running down his face and he looked like he was about to collapse.

"He's gone." He pointed a thumb over his shoulder. "That son of a bitch ran out the other door and is gone. I looked even down the stairs, but I can't see him anywhere. I can't believe I've just been outrun by a ninety year old man!" He hit the door frame with his fist.

Jia walked over and hugged him, hiding her face in his neck. He kissed her hair and looked at the scene in front of him.

Tseten had translated what Mike had said and two of the monks ran past Mike and after Yau. Several other monks had already begun to silently carry the boxes out of the room.

Mike saw the lower edge of an orange robe and two sandaled feet disappear in the chimney. Two more were kneeling next to Zhou and when one of them touched Zhou's face, he jerked and started coughing.

The young man who had saved Karen still stood in the middle of the room, looking at Dean and Karen with a wide smile on his face.

"WHERE DO THEY bring the spheres?"
Tseten turned to Mike. "We have place, very near. It is safe."
Lightning flashed outside and for a moment a frozen picture of the wind-swept Suzhou Creek appeared in the windows. Heavy thunder rumbled through the city.
"It will take you all night to remove the gold. After what just happened, the police may come any minute!"
"We take only the spheres and... papers?"
"The scrolls?"

"Yes. Spheres and scrolls. Gold is not important." Tseten gave a quick smile, aware of what he had just said.

"Now that is a refreshing thought. What was Yau looking for? He seemed to search for some special item."

Tseten shrugged. "He did research. He knows about spheres. Each sphere is... different?" He struggled with the words. "Has a different effect. He is very old. Some spheres can help."

Mike slowly nodded with his mouth open, processing the immensity of the information he had just received. He replied slowly, whispering to himself. "He is old and the spheres can help. Oh my god!"

MEANWHILE IN THE background more than a dozen monks were transporting a stream of boxes from the chimney out of the room. They were working in complete silence and while their movements never seemed hurried, they were moving at speeds beyond what a human being should be capable of. Mike, Dean, Jia and Karen watched in awe.

Dean turned to Mike. "We have to find Yau."

"He should be halfway to the airport by now. If he bolts to Hong Kong, we are in deep trouble. But I don't think so. He's too well known there. He knows his son will be arrested or is dead, he still has not found the sphere he's looking for and his hand is messed up. He'll be heading for the hills. His hills."

Dean slowly nodded. "I think you are right... he still wants what we have. And he wants us dead."

They were contemplating this thought in silence when the sound of sirens became audible above the thunder of the storm, first very low, but becoming louder with every second.

KAREN LOOKED FOR Tseten. He held several long boxes with documents in his arms and was about to turn away.

"Tseten! We already have rooms here in the hotel – you can hide there!"

Tseten bowed. "No. We have save place." With that he turned and left the room. Dean and Kun helped Zhou to his feet and the six of them left room 517.

The door to Jia and Mike's suite stood open when they arrived on their side of the fifth floor. They barely had time to close the door behind them before they could hear the heavy steps of police officers running up the stairs.

The box made of dark wood was gone.

53

THERE WAS INDEED an airfield near Jinshi. After the second world war the Chinese Army had built the airfield by dynamiting large parts of a hill and shoveling the resulting rubble into the neighboring valley. It was a long strip of asphalt surrounded by low hills with a small, squat tower and a half dozen hangars that had already been rusting at the dawn of the jet age.

The military still owned this monument to cracked concrete and rusty corrugated steel, but for decades only a few crop dusters had taken off from here. Three soldiers, largely forgotten by the world, manned the tower during daytime, spending most of their time as if stranded on an uninhabited island.

But now with the economic boom a new kind of bird had begun to flock here – private jets that could be chartered out of the metropolitan centers landed here frequently, flying in with newly rich Chinese businessmen who came to inspect their holdings in the far-flung Hunan and Hubei provinces.

One such jet was now bouncing and rattling along the asphalt runway with its thrust reversers screaming, then finally settling down to a smooth roll that ended with a short squeak of the breaks near the airport tower.

A DOOR ON the sleek, blue and white jet opened and a set of gangway stairs unfolded in a silent ballet of mechanical parts.

Dean's head appeared through the door. He turned back. "You've got to be kidding me! It's even more humid here than back in Shanghai!"

He stepped down the stairs, wearing blue jeans and a white, short-sleeved shirt. He was carrying two black leather briefcases and had a small backpack on his shoulders. He was followed by Karen, Jia and Mike, all of them in casual clothes and backpacks, and all of them carrying identical briefcases.

A Chinese-made Jeep SUV rolled to a stop next to the plane and the driver came out to greet them. He was a short man with a round, friendly face. His eyebrows were thick and bushy and seemed to live independent lives, always in motion, but almost never agreeing with each other on what to do. Currently the right eyebrow was up.

"Welcome to Jinshi. My name is Huo Beijiang and I work for Shanghai Security Associates." He shook Dean's hand and gave a curt bow to the two women and Mike. He turned around and opened the back of the Jeep for their luggage.

WHILE THEY STOWED their briefcases and bags, Mike stepped away from the Jeep and took a quick survey of the airfield. There was one other jet parked far on the other side of the airfield in the shadows of one of the rusty hangars, the engine openings closed to the elements with white plastic covers. Two men in dark blue suits with their jackets removed sat next to the open door of the jet on white lawn chairs, reading newspapers and glancing at the new arrivals as their only escape from boredom. Mike noted that this jet was parked so that it could not be seen by the soldiers in the tower of the airfield.

The hills that they had seen uncomfortably close from the descending airplane were rounded knobs of rock densely overgrown with bamboo and low bushes. There were no sounds of human activity and all he could hear were the grinding noises of bamboo stalks rubbing against each other in the warm mid-day wind, interrupted by bursts of noise from the local cicada population.

Mike slowly turned on his heels and used his arm to shield his eyes. The midday sun was beating down on them mercilessly from a bright blue sky and the air was so humid, that Mike felt like he was walking through a steam bath.

The only sign of civilization outside of the fence that Mike could see was the one road that connected this airfield with the rest of the world.

Their pilot slowly walked around the airplane for a quick check and then entered the plane again and closed the door. Moments later the engines on both sides of the tail of the airplane came alive with a slow whine that turned higher with every second. The plane taxied around away from the SUV. When it reached the end of the runway the whine turned into a roar and the plane accelerated. It vaulted into the blue sky at a steep angle to avoid the bamboo groves on the hills, banked and vanished in a small black dot. All around, cicadas returned to their songs.

THE FRIENDS AND Huo climbed into the hulking Jeep Grand Cherokee and for a moment just sat there and enjoyed the cool air from the air conditioner wafting around their sweaty bodies. Then Huo followed the bumpy road away from the airfield.

Their first stop was a guest house outside of Jinshi at the shore of a small lake. Huo had already booked rooms for the two couples and to their delight they found that nobody else was staying in the rambling collection of small bungalows that lined the lake. For a long time this had been a hangout for local officials of the communist party, but it had seen a drastic decline in popularity now that Chinese were allowed to spend their vacations out of the country.

DEAN AND KAREN stood on a short wooden dock that hosted a small fleet of rowboats that had seen better days. They had all taken a break in their rooms, snoozed and taken cold showers to at least momentarily escape from the heat. Before they had to continue on their trip into the hills, Dean and Karen snuck away for a short walk.

"They took you past this lake only a week ago."

Karen turned back from the lake and took both of his hands in hers. She leaned back and their arms stretched between them.

"It already sounds so unbelievably strange. I was a hostage, blindfolded, scared. So many things have happened since then, it feels like it was a year ago."

"Not that we need that information to find Yau, but do you remember anything about the drive?"

"It took a long time and the road wasn't good. Lot's of bumps and the driver was swerving a lot. And the air was incredible, fresh and full of the smell of trees."

"How about the path up to the temple?"

"It was pitch black most of the time. I just followed Tseten wherever he went. He often had to take my hand since I would have lost him in the dark forest. I should be able to find them with our map. It doesn't match what I remember exactly, but there is really only one hill with an ancient temple on the top that could be the one. I've spent quite some time with that map and I'm pretty confident."

"Well then, it's time to go"

BACK IN THE Jeep Dean was sitting in front, giving the driver of the Jeep directions. Over the last few days they had made contact with Helen Turner again and she had found detailed maps of the area around Jinshi. Through her contacts at the History Department of the Shanghai University she had been able to pinpoint the location of Martin Yau's inherited land.

They drove along a bumpy road that slowly wound its way around several heavily wooded hills, all the time gaining altitude.

"So... Dean. You still don't want to talk about that idea of yours?"

Dean turned back in the passenger seat and looked at his friends. "No. Not really. It would be different if I had more information about the Guardians and the spheres. But until we talk to them I honestly don't know what we can do about Yau."

"But you said you had an idea." Jia was pouting at him.

"Yes. And I could be horribly wrong. Let me talk to them first."

AFTER HALF AN hour they reached a fork in the road and they stopped.

"OK, this is your stop!" Dean turned back to Mike and Jia.

"I hope your were holding the map the right way up. I don't want to be stranded out here. You know, I've heard stories in Shanghai that there's still some wild tigers up in these mountains."

Jia laughed. "Fat chance of seeing one of those. I'd be more worried about us running into one of Yau's people."

She opened the door and climbed out. "Well then, see you later. I promise to protect Mike from the tigers."

Mike followed her and pulled their backpacks out after him.

"Wow. These are heavy! Honey, what did you pack in there?"

"Food. A girl has to eat." Jia smiled impishly and gave him a quick kiss.

"See you later. Good luck up in the hills!" Mike pushed the back door shut.

KAREN WAVED AT them as the Jeep pulled away. She laughed and leaned forward, putting her hands on Dean's shoulders. "They are a fun couple. And completely unflappable. Have you ever seen them stressed out?"

Dean turned back to her. "No. They don't do stress."

Huo had turned the Jeep off the main road and they were now driving up a narrow forestry road that became more and more rough and after about a mile had lost all resemblance of a real road and turned into a dirt track. After another mile, Huo found a place where the path widened enough for him to turn around. He stopped the Jeep and shut down the engine.

"According to the map, the trail head should be only several hundred meters ahead from here. I will keep my walkie talkie on and wait for about half an hour before I return to the guest house, but I don't know if we will be able to reach each other in this terrain."

Dean and Karen got out of the Jeep and put their backpacks on. Dean nodded at Huo. "See you... well, when we are done. We'll call you on the satellite phone when we are ready for a pick up." He closed the door.

THEY BOTH WORE good hiking boots and the path had been drying out after the last rain, so the walking was not too rough. The air felt fresher than down at the airfield and a light breeze helped them to avoid overheating. After only twenty minutes they had found the narrow trail as it snaked its way up into the hills.

Karen pointed up into the trees along the steep flank of the hill.

"If we follow this trail we should be hitting the path that I and Tseten used that night. I'd say about an hour's worth of hiking from here."

Dean looked up the hill where the path was just a slight indentation in the forest floor, covered by dry leaves and riddled with roots. "Wow. I don't know how he did that in the middle of the night. Even now in the sun it is hard to see where the trail is."

"Yeah. I have no idea how he did that. And he was so sure about it too. The whole time while we were walking he never as much as stopped to find his way. The only thing slowing him down was me."

They started the serious part of their hike, making slow progress along the trail. Several times they had to turn back and try a different direction when the trail dissolved into chaotic loops with faint traces of foot steps leading in different directions.

FINALLY THEY MADE it to the top of a ridge that followed a row of hills. Dean took his backpack off and stretched.

"That last part was pretty steep. And look over there! That's the path coming up from Yau's estate. From here on it should be easier going." He pulled out a small GPS receiver and checked their coordinates on the map.

"And we've made it to the right spot, too. Shouldn't be more than another hour or so to the temple."

Karen was still out of breath. She was leaning against a tree with her backpack and took deep gulps from a water bottle. Sweat dropped off her nose.

"It was for sure easier to do this during a cool night. This humidity is a killer!" She straightened up and walked over to the path that followed the ridge. "Let's go. If I sit down now, you'll have to carry me."

54

JIA WAS CROUCHED down, pressing binoculars against her eyes. She tried to control her breathing to steady her view of the buildings below her.

"There he is. Yau just came out of the main building again. For a moment I saw him in the courtyard before he disappeared." She lowered the binoculars and grinned at Mike who was straddling a fallen tree behind her. He was eating a sandwich, completely at peace with the world.

"Did you notice anything about him?"

"Yeah, like you said... He looks different. There is the hand, of course, but he seems to walk differently, too. Almost like his son used to walk. It's too far away to see his features clearly, but I think he is using that sphere."

"Yeah, I still can't believe that this is actually possible. But at the end, that's what it is all about. Eternal youth."

Jia shrugged. "It may not have been a big deal when he was still young after the war and he was probably thinking more about the gold he had lost, but over the years the power of these spheres must have become an obsession with him. Here he was, one of the most powerful people in Hong Kong, getting older and older. And he knew that at one point he had held the key to living forever and it had been stolen from under his nose!"

Mike was done with the sandwich and leaned back against the tree. He closed his eyes while Jia turned back to fulfill her half-hour shift with the binoculars.

From time to time Jia took a notebook and completed a small map she had created of Yau's compound. She marked the building where she thought Yau was staying.

IT WAS GETTING dark when they set up a small tent under the trees, out of view from Yau's house. Their observations had mostly served to establish a general pattern of activity for Yau, but as they had expected, he was still recuperating and would not move anytime soon. He seemed to only have the smooth-talker and one bodyguard with him in his residence. There was no reason to stay awake all night.

Mike had rolled out a large camping mattress in their tent and had stowed all the gear in one corner. His head came back out of the tent, only to be met by a kiss from Jia. She pushed him back into the tent, followed him in and with one smooth motion closed the door zipper behind her.

55

DEAN STOPPED.

The sun had disappeared behind the hills and shadows dominated the forest around them. The path in front of them ended under the curved eaves of temple ruins, and there was dark red light emanating from a building straight ahead.

Karen had been hiking along behind Dean, deep in thought. She now bumped into his backpack and sidestepped to prevent a fall.

"What is it?" Her eyes focused on what was before them. "Oh!"

"We've arrived." Dean slowly stepped across a raised stone threshold into the courtyard.

Karen walked past him and pointed to her left. "This is where I sat when I was talking to the monks! It is so strange to see this with a little more light. Let's go and see if we can find them!"

Dean wasn't so sure anymore if this had been a good idea. But now was not the time for self-doubt. He followed her deeper into the temple complex.

Karen slowly walked up the steps of the building in front of them. "The incense smells so good!"

SHE TURNED TO Dean with a smile and froze. Dean was walking up the steps, looking down to avoid stumbling on the uneven stones. Behind him stood two monks in orange robes as if they had always been there, their arms at their sides. Karen had seen this stance before and by now recognized it as the Guardian's preferred position at the beginning of combat.

"Dean! Stop!"

"What?"

He looked up and stopped, one foot a step higher than the other. He saw her face and slowly turned his head, following her stare.

"Oops." He took another step to stabilize himself and turned around to face the monks.

THEY HAD TALKED about this moment and had decided for Karen to speak first.

"Uhm... Hi! My name is Karen and this is Dean. We are friends. I have been here before, one week ago. With Tseten."

Tseten's name caused a reaction. The two men looked at each other and one of them jogged silently away and around the corner. The other one just stood there, unmoving.

A moment later Tseten came around the corner, out of breath. He looked at them, his eyes reflecting the red light from the temple.

"Karen? Why here?" Behind him, more monks came around the corner and the low murmur of their voices filled the courtyard.

"Nice to see you again, Tseten. We have a proposal for the Guardians of Time. You help us, we help you."

SEVERAL MINUTES LATER they were sitting crosslegged in one of the halls of the temple. It was a long, empty hall with several large rugs layered over each other. A low table in the middle was surrounded by cushions to sit on. They were slurping green tea from small, elegant cups served by one of the monks. Tseten sat at their side in his new role as their liaison, while the old monk Karen had spoken to a week ago sat across the table.

"Miss Chadbourne, Mr. Lashure. I'm not overstating anything if I say that it is a surprise to see you here." The old monk had brown, leathery skin and his kind eyes left the impression that their owner had seen the world and approved of it. He had short salt and pepper hair that was receding over his temples.

Karen nodded. "We are sorry to disturb you here, but we have a proposal to make that will allow us to restore our normal lives. In return, the Guardians of Time will recoup at least some of their financial losses from the lost gold. You may have heard that the Shanghai Police found the gold that was still in the attic above room 517 in the Suzhou Hotel. But they did not find everything. We had removed several million dollars worth of gold from the attic before Martin Yau found us."

She took a sip from the strong tea. Even in the heat of this summer night there was steam rising from the cup, playing around her hair.

Dean used the break to open his backpack. "And before we discuss the rest of our plan, I would like to give you back several artifacts that we had also removed from the attic."

He pulled the two boxes with the first two spheres they had recovered from the backpack and gently sat them down on the table. Then he loosened the fabric loops on the side of the backpack and lifted the three slender document boxes out of the embrace of the loops, setting them down on top of the two boxes with the spheres.

Tseten stood up, took the boxes and solemnly carried them out of the room.

"THANK YOU FOR returning our property. We are forever indebted to you. But surely you are not carrying the gold bars with you?" A smile played around his lips.

"No... but we can pay you a fair market price for the gold we have removed, minus a few expenses we incurred during this operation. The money is in this other backpack." Karen gave Dean a quick sidelong glance. "But first a few questions."

Dean sat up straight and took a deep breath. "We would like to know who the Guardians are. You have returned the woman I love to me, and you have rescued us from almost certain death by Yau. But it is possible that we are just pawns in this game and that you are at the end no better than Yau and his Triad. We need an explanation for what happened to us, and why."

The old man drank some tea and then sat there for several moments, staring at the leaves in his cup as they were slowly swirling around. He closed his eyes for a moment and took a deep breath. Then he turned back to his guests and smiled.

"Yes, I think you have earned yourself an explanation."

Another long silence. He looked deep into Karen's and Dean's eyes.

"WE ARE THE Guardians of Time. Our order is very small and only a few people know about us. But we are an old order. Very old. More than two thousand years ago, a goldsmith at the court of the Chinese Emperor discovered a new way to create thinner and thinner spheres of gold. He noticed that with certain other enhancements, he could create these spheres inside of each other, and so he tried to do just that. It was supposed to be nothing more than artwork, beautiful things made to the greater glory of the Emperor."

"After many years of experimentation, when he finally succeeded to create the first of these... spheres within spheres, something unexpected happened. When he spun these spheres, *time changed.*"

"The goldsmith was in panic. His work for the emperor was supposed to produce works of art, but he had created a machine that had disturbing effects... he was afraid of the court eunuchs discovering what he had done. They would immediately be suspicious of his motives. Did he want to harm the imperial family? Aimless suspicions grew in the imperial court like weeds."

"His brother was a monk in a small, remote monastery and the goldsmith went there to ask for advice. Eventually he smuggled all of the spheres out of the palace and to the monastery. For the next two thousand years our order has been researching the effects of the spheres and how to control them. We kept them out of the hands of a long succession of either ignorant or blood-thirsty emperors. We became the guardians of these spheres."

DEAN CLEARED HIS throat. "Yau seems to know something about how these spheres work. He has now one of the spheres that was kept in a different box than all the others."

"Yes. Martin Yau. He and his father were the only ones who uncovered our secrets in all these years. He is a very dangerous man."

"So... the sphere he was so desperate to recover. It can... change him?"

The old monk's eyes had turned narrow. "The spheres are very powerful."

Dean kept on looking at the man in front of them. "Very powerful indeed. Why was Yau so desperate? Why was this one sphere marked differently? Why had he risked to come to Shanghai himself? He is old and will die soon – what could this sphere offer that makes all of this worth to him?"

"There's only one answer. This specific sphere can keep him alive, maybe even rejuvenate him."

Dean's eyes never left the monk's expressionless face. "Was it *your* brother who brought the spheres to the monastery?"

KAREN'S EYES REFLECTED the candlelight around them. She looked back and forward between Dean and the monk. "What? Are you nuts? That happened two thousand years ago!"

"Yes." The monk never took his eyes from Dean's.

"Wha..." Karen's mouth opened and closed in shock.

Dean nodded slowly. He took Karen's hand in his and squeezed it. They both examined the face of the man in front of them with new eyes. It was a large, friendly face with dark, sunburnt skin and slightly Tibetan features. Many small wrinkles surrounded the eyes, but he looked no older than maybe sixty years of age.

Karen shook her head. "No way. I don't believe any of this. So how old is Tseten? A thousand years?"

The monk smiled gently. "No. He is nineteen. He is our youngest apprentice."

Karen was shaking her head. "But... but how does this work? You spin the spheres and what? Time stops?"

"It depends on the sphere. My brother made many different versions of these spheres and only a few have positive effects. Many of them are very dangerous and we keep them buried. But some can be used to change the flow of time in a small area around them. *Stop* time. *Turn* it. We have spent thousands of years studying how time works and what the spheres do, but there are still some that we do not understand at all."

Karen shook her head. "But I've seen Tseten do some amazing things in a fight where he was not even near one of the spheres."

"Exposure to the spheres and their effects changes us. Time becomes something like water streaming past our minds. We can influence reality around us for some very short moments, even without the help of the artifacts."

"So your brother is also still alive?"

"No... he died when the last sphere he made *accelerated* the time around him."

Karen looked down. "I'm sorry."

"Oh, no... that was a very, very long time ago. But no new spheres have been made ever since."

DEAN WAS INTRIGUED. "Accelerated time? Do these spheres all look very similar? The ones I have seen looked all the same to me."

"The inscriptions are different and the size and shape of the holes in the spheres are slightly different. But essentially the spheres are nearly identical. There have been accidents when inexperienced members of our order have experimented with them. Why?"

Karen raised her hand to her mouth. She now fully understood what Dean had been planning all along. They had come here with a vague notion of somehow stopping Yau, and Dean had implied that he had an idea that would need the help of the Guardians. And now she knew.

"Oh my god!"

Dean nodded at her. Then he turned back to the old man. "Yau will be getting stronger and he saw Guardians kill his son. He will come after your order if he is not stopped. I have an idea that will take care of Yau. For good – and both for us and you. But I will need your help."

"You are right. He is going to be a growing menace to us. How can we help?"

56

THE WALKIE TALKIE crackled to life. "Mike? This is Dean."

Mike woke up, tried to get up and hit his head on the tent pole. The memory of last night returned and he realized where he was. He scrambled to find a flash light in the darkness. Finally he found the light and switched it on. Jia turned on her back and sleepily held a hand in front of her eyes. Mike grabbed the walkie talkie and hit the button.

"Dean? Where are you?"

"Halfway down the trail that leads to the back of the house. And where are you?"

"We put our tent up out of view of the house behind a small ridge, about two hundred yards up the hill. We couldn't find the trail yesterday evening, but I'd estimate we are not more than thirty or forty yards to the east of it. How did it go?"

"Very good. We found the temple and we've struck a deal. We should be in your neighborhood in another half hour or so. Is Yau still there?"

"Yep. Just come down. He should be slumbering peacefully right now."

It was just after five o'clock when Jia and Mike heard a low voice and twigs breaking nearby. They had spent the meantime to fold up the tent and clear their camp. Mike switched on the walkie talkie. He whispered into it. "That better be you!"

"Yes." Came the muffled answer back.

"We can hear you just to our west. Stop right there and we'll find you."

A FIRST, VERY soft pre-dawn glow was visible in the east and it was enough for Jia and Mike to avoid running into trees. A minute later they hugged and shook hands with Karen and Dean. Mike was relieved to see his friends. "Dr. Lashure, I presume."

Dean had to suppress his laughter. "Not a doctor by a long shot. You already know Tseten."

Mike shook Tseten's hand. The young man gave him a firm handshake and smiled back at him.

"Mike, could you see who is with Yau?"

"Yes, he has only one bodyguard and the smooth-talking bastard with him and they are staying in different buildings." He nodded at Jia.

She took her map of Yau's compound out of a pocket and showed it to the others in the dark blue light of the beginning dawn. "The bodyguard sleeps in a room next to the main entrance, here. And just next to it is the room of the caretaker of the place, some harmless-looking dude."

"The Smoothtalker is staying here in the back of the courtyard in what looks like a little guest bungalow. And Yau is here to the south in the main building."

Karen pointed at the map. "And here in the back to the north is where I was locked up. We are now straight above that part of the compound."

She turned to Tseten who had been looking on, obviously interested in the map. "So, Tseten. Do you think you can do the switch without waking up everybody?"

"Yes. He will not hear me. This is easy."

DEAN OPENED HIS backpack and pulled the lid off a square box inside. He slowly lifted a golden sphere out of the box and held it up for everybody to see. The light of dawn, now with a first touch of pink, was amplified by the glossy polish of the sphere. It looked like pure energy was coming off the gold.

Mike was surprised. "Another sphere?"

"Yes. Remember when you wanted to know about my idea? This is it."

"What? You spin it up and throw it down into the compound?"

"Close, but no. We are not spinning it up. *Yau will.*"

DEAN SLOWLY AND carefully wrapped the sphere into a square piece of black silk and handed it with both hands to Tseten.

"Good Luck!"

Tseten took the sphere with both hands and bowed to Dean. "Thank you."

Without another word he turned and silently disappeared in the undergrowth of the bamboo forest.

JIA LOOKED THROUGH the binoculars and gave a whispered account of what she saw. She stood above her friends and her head was surrounded by the glorious colors of dawn.

"He just came out of Yau's side of the building and he is now crossing the courtyard."

"I can see him at the garden wall next to the guest bungalow. He jumped across. Clean, without a running start. That wall is at least seven feet high!"

Only ten minutes later Tseten had joined them behind the ridge. He nodded. "It is done."

He took a golden sphere from its silken wrapping, undistinguishable from the one he had carried down to Yau's house, and gently settled it into the box in Dean's backpack.

They settled down for a long wait.

IT WAS KAREN'S turn at the binoculars several hours later when Tseten suddenly looked up. His eyes were unnaturally big and for a moment only white was showing. He slumped forward again and was breathing heavily.

Mike got up. "A seizure?"

Karen looked back and held Mike's shoulder. "No. I've seen that before. Somebody is using a sphere."

She took the binoculars back up and peered over the ridge at Yau's house.

AND THEN THERE was the scream. They would never forget how the voice of Martin Yau suddenly filled the valley from hillside to hillside with terror. The forceful voice rang out and then turned into a feeble screech, echoing back from the hills.

Tseten caught his breath and looked at them. He got up.

"It is done."

"That was it?" Dean could not believe that their plan had actually worked.

"Yes. He has turned the sphere. He is not here anymore."

Karen had still been looking trough the binoculars. Now she turned back. "They have found him! The bodyguard... oh my god. He just came back out from the house and... he seems to be sick."

She dropped the binoculars around her neck and came down from the perch atop the ridge. She walked up to Tseten and hugged him. He hugged her back and then he took a step away from her.

Tseten bowed to them.

The friends bowed back to him. For a moment the forest was silent.

Tseten picked up Dean's backpack, turned away and slowly walked up through the forest.

"Good Bye, Tseten."

They heard his voice one more time. "Good Bye, Karen."

And with these words he disappeared.

THE END

About the Author

Thomas Sturm is a software engineer for a large interactive media agency in San Francisco and he lives in the Bay Area with his wife Kazumi and their son Luke Akira.

Previously he had worked in a video game store, earned a degree in Electrical Engineering, traveled the world, repaired washing machines, developed computer games and once helped write a multitasking operating system in a summer. He has also spent one year forty meters underground for the German Airforce, apparently fighting the mole people.

He can usually be found walking the streets of San Francisco with a vintage Kodak Medalist at the ready.

Shanghai Gold is his first novel.

www.ingramcontent.com/pod-product-compliance
Lightning Source LLC
Chambersburg PA
CBHW032101050726
47590CB00001B/367